BEING WHITE

EDITED BY DUNCAN GRAHAM

Sixteen 'whitefellas' explore their relationship with Aboriginal Australia, looking at events in their own lives which shaped their understanding and appreciation of Aboriginal culture and history. Each contributor has shown a strong interest in the concerns of Aboriginal Australians over many years.

In their lively, highly readable, and personal stories these writers share experiences and wrestle with the issues of today, from dispossession and disadvantage, through struggle, to achievement and celebration. Their accounts will, as Sir Ronald Wilson says in his Foreword, 'do much to promote understanding in all sections of the Australian community.'

If, through the frank observations and personal stories of the authors, this book helps you share the limitless mysteries of this land, to recognise the history great and mean, to forgive the wrongs and rejoice in the good fortune which has given us such beauty, bounty and common wealth, then another stage has been reached on the road to reconciliation.
Duncan Graham.

Cover painting: Robert Juniper, *Flight to Lennonville*, 1984, 183x138cm, mixed media on Belgian linen. Reproduced courtesy of the artist. (Photographed by Richard Woldendorp.)

BEING WHITEFELLA

BEING WHITEFELLA

edited by Duncan Graham

FREMANTLE ARTS CENTRE PRESS

First published 1994 by
FREMANTLE ARTS CENTRE PRESS
193 South Terrace (PO Box 320), South Fremantle
Western Australia, 6162.

Copyright compilation © Duncan Graham, 1994.
Copyright individual pieces © Individual contributors,1994.

This book is copyright. Apart from any fair dealing for the purpose of private study, research, criticism or review, as permitted under the Copyright Act, no part may be reproduced by any process without written permission.
Enquiries should be made to the publisher.

Consultant editor B R Coffey.
Designed by John Douglass.
Production Coordinator Tony George.

Typeset in Times by Fremantle Arts Centre Press and printed on 89 gsm Husky Bulky by Mercury Press, Perth.

National Library of Australia
Cataloguing-in-publication data

Being whitefella.

    ISBN 1 86368 080 2.

    [1.] Aborigines, Australian. [2.] Aborigines, Australian – Social conditions. I. Graham, 1938- .

305.89915.

The human metals melt and melting down
Strike fault in fault and shattering neath the steel
The two base metals scream a new appeal

(Kevin Gilbert: *Because a White Man'll Never Do It.*)

To Cameron.
One of the whitefellas who'll do it.

ACKNOWLEDGEMENTS

This book is underpinned by the support and inspiration of friends, particularly those in the Aboriginal-Media Liaison Group and family, particularly my wife and partner, Ann Graham.

The words of Archie Roach in chapter 7 are reproduced with permission.

Fremantle Arts Centre Press receives financial assistance from the Western Australian Department for the Arts.

CONTENTS

Foreword: Sir Ronald Wilson		11
Introduction: Duncan Graham		17
1 Bruce Petty	Try Listening to the Softer Voices	31
2 Teresa Ashforth	Different Ways of Talking	38
3 Fred Chaney	Too Many Mingy Buggers	50
4 Victoria Laurie	Cry for the Lost Chances	60
5 Ted Egan	Thinking in Australian	69
6 Diana Simmonds	Finding the Heart's Home	78
7 Hal Jackson	A Late Learning	84
8 Duncan Graham	No Questions Please, We're Australians	93
9 Kim Beazley	Oppression Doesn't Need another Race	110

10 Geoffrey Bolton	Portrait of the Historian as a Young Learner	119
11 Robert Juniper	Searching for a Black Ancestry	126
12 Veronica Brady	The Presence which is Absence	132
13 Bill Bunbury	A Long, Long Wait Time	145
14 Catherine H Berndt	Coloured Lenses and Social Relationships	151
15 Myrna Tonkinson	Thinking in Colour	162
16 Judith Wright	Being White Woman	177

| Notes on Contributors | 183 |
| Further Reading | 185 |

FOREWORD

Sir Ronald Wilson

There are at least two reasons why I'm writing the foreword. The first arises from my deep respect and affection for many Aboriginal people built up over almost twenty-five years of personal relationships. Those began with the New Era Aboriginal Fellowship (NEAF), an organisation whose membership was open to both Aboriginal and other Australians and which functioned throughout the 1970s.

Two of the highlights of NEAF's activities during those years were the establishment of both the Aboriginal Legal Service and the Aboriginal Medical Service, agencies which have since gone from strength to strength. The 1980s were marked by the emergence of the Uniting Aboriginal and Islander Christian Congress as a semi-autonomous body within the Uniting Church.

These years brought to me the privilege of visiting Aboriginal communities in Arnhem Land and the Pitjantjatjara country. Of course the relationships established during these years continue within the fellowship of the Church. The 1990s have brought with them fresh opportunities of working with Aboriginal people through the Human Rights and Equal Opportunity Commission and, more recently, the Council for Aboriginal Reconciliation.

Membership of the Council has proved in itself to be a most interesting experience in personal relationships. The Council has a membership of twenty-five people, twelve of whom are Aborigines, two are Torres Strait Islanders, and the remaining eleven other Australians. One of those is an immigrant of Chinese racial origin.

We began as twenty-five very different people reflecting a considerable diversity of background and life experiences. Yet we rapidly underwent a miniature process of reconciliation. Undoubtedly the factors that made this possible were the magnitude of the task given to us, the crucial importance of the outcome of that task to the future of the nation, and above all a common commitment to the process of reconciliation.

The bonding process was facilitated by the consensus reached at our first meeting on a form of words which represented the vision of the Council. This vision has since served both to remind us of our task and to provide a yardstick by which to measure the response of the community. That vision is of:

> A united Australia which values this land of ours, which respects its Aboriginal and Torres Strait Islander heritage, and which provides justice and equity for all.

I spoke of two reasons which encouraged me to accept the invitation to write this foreword. The second is the importance of *Being Whitefella* to this process of reconciliation. To show how and why this is so, it is desirable first to discuss the reconciliation process.

This got off to a great start with multi-party support for its legislative vehicle, the Council for Aboriginal Reconciliation Act 1991. The significance of the unanimous support from the Commonwealth Parliament finds emphasis in the affirmations contained in the Preamble to the Act. These affirmations are so important that they deserve to be cited in full:

> Because:
> (a) Australia was occupied by Aborigines and Torres Strait Islanders who had settled for thousands of years, before British settlement at Sydney Cove on 26 January 1788; and
> (b) many Aborigines and Torres Strait Islanders suffered dispossession and dispersal from their traditional lands by the British Crown; and
> (c) to date, there has been no formal process of reconciliation

between Aborigines and Torres Strait Islanders and other Australians; and

(d) by the year 2001, the centenary of Federation, it is most desirable that there be such a reconciliation; and

(e) as a part of the reconciliation process, the Commonwealth will seek an ongoing national commitment from governments at all levels to co-operate and to co-ordinate with the Aboriginal and Torres Strait Island Commission as appropriate to address progressively Aboriginal disadvantage and aspirations in relation to land, housing, law and justice, cultural heritage, education, employment, health, infrastructure, economic development and any other relevant matters in the decade leading to the centenary of Federation, 2001.

The Parliament of Australia therefore enacts: ...

The object of the Act is described in section 5 as follows :

The object of the establishment of the Council is to promote a process of reconciliation between Aborigines and Torres Strait Islanders and the wider Australian community, based on an appreciation by the Australian community as a whole of Aboriginal and Torres Strait Islander cultures and achievements, and of the unique position of Aborigines and Torres Strait Islanders as the indigenous peoples of Australia, and by means that include the fostering of an ongoing national commitment to co-operate to address Aboriginal and Torres Strait Islander disadvantage.

It can be seen that the truths recorded in (a) and (b) of the Preamble have since formed the basis of the High Court ruling that the common law of Australia recognises that, unless extinguished, traditional rights in relation to land, (described as native title) resides in the traditional owners.

These affirmations can no longer be dismissed as political rhetoric. They are embodied in the law of the land. The decision is of enormous significance to the reconciliation process. Before the decision the claims and aspirations of indigenous Australians represented an appeal to the goodwill and sense of justice of other Australians. Now those claims and aspirations have the backing of historical legal right.

The decision is also important in a symbolic way, building in indigenous peoples a sense of self-respect and a rightful claim to equality in negotiations over a just and proper settlement which takes account of the dispossession and other injustices of the past and present. Of course, much may depend on the capacity of our legislators to respond to the decision in a way which honours justice and truth.

It will be seen from the passages from the statute that I've quoted that the essence of the process of reconciliation is to lead the whole nation, both indigenous and other Australians, to recognise that if we are to share this country as a united people there is not only a need for change but that individual Australians must be prepared to work for the necessary change.

The Council for Aboriginal Reconciliation believes that this recognition of the need for change, and for individual commitment to pursue that change, will come as all Australians gain understanding.

It's an understanding not only of the relevant issues but also of one another, our hopes and fears, the paths we've travelled and our appreciations of the common future that awaits us. The programs followed so far are designed to communicate and to consult, both with indigenous communities and with the wider community.

The outcomes of these programs will be reported to a National Consultation to be held towards the end of 1994.

In the meantime, much progress is being made in building bridges between Aboriginal leaders and leaders in the different sectors of Australian business activity. Promising relationships are being established between Aboriginal leaders and the peak bodies representing farmers, pastoralists and people in the cattle industry. The trade union movement and the Australian Chamber of Commerce and Industry are each devoting attention to issues of Aboriginal employment and codes of conduct directed to the elimination of racism within the workforce.

These various developments, coupled, of course, with the ongoing work of the Race Discrimination Commissioner and the Aboriginal Social Justice Commissioner, both of whom are members of the National Human Rights and Equal Opportunity Commission, encourage me to hope that Australia can rid itself of the shackles of racism in the remaining years of this decade.

I believe that an important way to promote understanding, probably the best way, is to encourage the telling of stories. In the case of many Aboriginal people the stories are of a recent history largely concerned with suffering, humiliation and disadvantage. Yet there are also stories of joy and hope, the kind of unquenchable optimism so well conveyed by the television documentary *Exile and the Kingdom*.

We non-indigenous Australians, we whitefellas, also have our stories drawn from our relationships with the former owners of our country. They may be stories of sorrow, of shame and embarrassment, but also of the joy of adventures shared together, of shared struggle and achievements, of pride in indigenous art, music and writing which now forms part of our culture.

This is where *Being Whitefella* is so special. The editor, Duncan Graham, is to be congratulated on the range and calibre of the essayists he's drawn together. Their testimonies and their stories will do much to promote understanding in all sections of the Australian community, including that significant number of Australians who have joined us in this country in recent decades and who have contributed so much to our cultural diversity.

It is therefore with a great deal of pleasure and anticipation that I welcome *Being Whitefella*. I believe it will be influential in the building of a united Australia.

Ronald Wilson
President, Human Rights and Equal Opportunity Commission
Deputy Chairperson, Council for Aboriginal Reconciliation
Chancellor, Murdoch University

INTRODUCTION

The genesis of *Being Whitefella* is in Aotearoa, which most Australians know as New Zealand. Of the 3.5 million people in that overpoweringly beautiful country with the ugliest towns outside East Germany and the world's best ice-cream, more than 500,000, or 16 per cent, are Maori, the people who were there when Cook arrived in 1769.

From 1788, when the British started a penal colony in New South Wales, European traders began exploiting the seals, flax and timber across the Tasman. To do so they had to deal with the Maori who were keen to obtain metal goods, including guns, and who controlled most landing places.

The almost total destruction of the indigenous people of Australia by the invaders was not duplicated in Aotearoa. In that land the country was more difficult to colonise, and the Maori well organised to resist invasion with military skills developed through centuries of inter-tribal warfare.

On 5 February 1840 the British signed the Treaty of Waitangi with Maori chiefs. Every year the event is celebrated and the complex rituals of Maori greeting and meeting protocol are recognised by national leaders. In Australia today the idea of any sort of compact with Aboriginal people is one of the nation's most contentious issues.

In the past ten years the Maori renaissance has ensured the one language lives with a vigour unimagined in Australia where more than half the original 250 distinct languages have disappeared, and the rest struggle to survive.

Maori still own large tracts of their own country despite the land deals of last century. They exercise political, legal and economic power, much of it hard-welded into the nation's constitution. For the most part Aboriginal people remain welfare dependent and politically powerless in the country they owned, managed, occupied and conserved for at least 50,000 years.

While Australia has prospered and grown to become a nation of more than 17 million following huge immigration programs and the discovery of vast natural resources, Aotearoa has remained small and apart. Aboriginal people have been swamped by the invaders and now form less than 1.5 per cent of the population, about 270,000 in all. There are almost as many members of the Returned Services League than there are Aboriginal people, and to appreciate the significance of that comment you'll have to read Chapter 6. That powerful lobby has a grand slogan: Lest We Forget. Curiously it's a maxim not allowed Aboriginal people who are forever urged to forget the past.

Yet despite these differences between our countries, and more than 200 years after the *Endeavour* sailed round the islands of Aotearoa and up the east coast of Australia, there are many similarities in the way the two nations handle relations between the races. Most are tragic.

More than half the people in Aotearoa's gaols are Maori. In Australia Aborigines fill the nation's prisons at a similarly disproportionate rate. To be a Maori is to be prone to poverty, unemployment and disease, to have a shortened life expectancy, a poorer education and less of a fair go. It's the same for Aboriginal Australians, though more so.

Racism is alive and well in both countries, though less likely to be up front in Aotearoa where the chances of causing offence and suffering its consequences are proportionately higher.

What is significantly different is the way the debate is handled. In Aotearoa the quest for identity by Pakeha, the newcomers, the later arrivals, appeared to me to be well articulated, a healthy robust discussion which lifted some of the racist rocks to let the scorpions of bigotry scuttle away. Much of the energy was being directed by Michael King, a Pakeha journalist turned academic and prolific author on things Maori.

In 1985 he published his biography *Being Pakeha*, somewhat presumptuous for a man only forty, but it gave the debate about being a New Zealander a nudge. Six years later Dr King edited a collection of essays written by academics, journalists, historians and others. He described this as:

> ... a continuation and extension of a journey I began in *Being Pakeha*. It is a series of personal explorations of the origins, metamorphoses and current state of an evolving culture in New Zealand.

Away from Aotearoa's most marvellous bookshops, though equally impactful, was the discovery of the words 'tane' and 'wahine' on the separate doors of a public toilet when I was in urgent need of that convenience, and no silly silhouette of a stylised male or female to guide decision-making. While enjoying the relief after making the right choice it struck me that any society which used the language of a minority was recognising a bicultural community. The widespread use of Maori words like mana (spiritual power or authority), tapu (sacred) and marae (space before a meeting house) in the mainstream press without translation is another indicator of a cultural merging unknown in Australia.

Dr King's anthology is called *Pakeha* and till now we've had nothing quite like it in Australia. In this country the quest for identity seems to be more concerned with the defeat at Gallipoli, myths of mateship and the outback, colonial and convict origins and, more recently, multi-culturalism. Despite the plurality of modern Australian society and regular reminders of our proximity to Asia, this country remains essentially European in outlook.

The internal symbols of our culture have ranged from broad-brimmed hats to Vietnamese cuisine, our icons from Ned Kelly to Manning Clark. From all these, Aboriginal people are either excluded or appear as fringe figures, exotic, dangerous and most certainly impossible to comprehend. Meanwhile Australia is promoted overseas through celebratory television commercials applauding dot paintings and corroborees.

The questions asked by most Australians seeking an understanding of the shape and texture of our nation's culture seem to hang on past ties with Britain. This is best exemplified in the debate on republicanism overlaid with calls to develop future links with Asia, an issue largely driven by economists. In both cases we are looking outside, seeking to prove ourselves by association with others. Yet the questions asked by visitors relate to Aboriginal culture and the way the races mix, not whether we intend producing PVC pipe fittings for Bangkok condominiums.

When the country's indigenous people and culture are discussed inside Australia it tends to be in negative terms, a problem, a threat. The High Court's 1992 decision to recognise native title released an ugly flood of invective, myths mouldy with age, ancient hates springing from old-brain fears. It was a them-and-us response, demonstrating yet again how long and rugged the track ahead to a land of harmony, justice and equality. It also begat the most gymnastic verbal contortions. 'Native title' became a 'bundle of rights' and these did not include ownership in the way understood by those with freehold title.

(The regular publication of the distressing statistics on Aboriginal morbidity and mortality encourage rednecks to believe the 'dying pillow' syndrome of the 1930's is still in place. They expected the indigenous people of this country will either die out or merge into invisibility through intermarriage, thereby eliminating the need to bother with Aboriginal concerns. Not so. Australian Bureau of Statistics figures show that the percentage increase in the number of Aboriginal people in Australia was 17 per cent between 1986 and 1991. This was more than double the increase for the total Australian population. Against this compare the ugly statistics of child mortality where perinatal deaths [up to one year] are five times greater if the babe is brown.)

When asking selected people with a known interest in the area to contribute to *Being Whitefella* I said:

Reconciliation is on the agenda of both major political parties at the federal level. There's a growing interest (or disquiet) about things Aboriginal. The Mabo case has raised serious questions about who owns the land. Issues of human rights and racism feature prominently in the media. The impact of the Royal Commission into Aboriginal Deaths in Custody is still being felt.

The issues I want the book (but not each essay) to examine include:

* How the writer rationalises her or his use of the land.
* The naming of non-Aboriginal Australians. (Identification through what a person is not, rather than what they are.)
* 'Some of my best friends are black.' Can an Aboriginal person be a pioneer, a 'forefather', a settler, a mate?
* Should we be bicultural before becoming multicultural? Can Aboriginal culture survive in a multicultural society?
* Is guilt an appropriate emotion to respond to the wrongs of the past? If not, what is?
* Responses to racism, and suggestions for change. Have political reactions and legislation had any positive effect? What role has the media taken?
* What Australian institutions, myths and values need to change if reconciliation is to succeed?
* Should there be a treaty? If so, what should it say? How could it be implemented? What practical effect would result?
* Reactions of successive Federal and State governments to Aboriginal concerns. Where has the pressure come from? State rights and human rights; which comes first?
* Do Aboriginal languages taught in schools have anything more than gimmick value? What can Aboriginal culture offer a society which has inherited Shakespeare, Christianity and democracy?
* Settlers or invaders? The language of history and the victors, and how this has influenced our thinking.
* The 'beautiful people' syndrome: are race relations still too sensitive to withstand objective criticism of things Aboriginal?

How often do we find ourselves saying the 'correct' thing about Aboriginal issues rather than the truth?
* Aborigines in literature: curios or real people? Have some aspects of Aboriginal culture been romanticised to make them acceptable?
* What enduring values can Aboriginal culture provide? Do these have to be embraced by other Australians?
* Can we be Australians without recognising Aboriginal land ownership?

I wanted to know how some people have become enmeshed in the issues, why they've stayed the course. I asked for the tone of the contributions to be personal and revealing rather than objective and academic. Apart from analysis and suggested resolutions I wanted to see these questions answered:

When did the writer first become aware of Aboriginal occupancy of Australia? What encounters has he or she had with Aboriginal people and culture? Substantial or fleeting? How has it affected them?

How have the writers coped with some of the above questions? Has support for Aboriginal concerns cost them friendships and promotion? What do they dislike about some Aboriginal approaches to political issues?

How well have we succeeded? That's for you to judge, but when you do, please appreciate that this was one of the toughest assignments most of the contributors have tackled, and that includes well-seasoned writers who make their livings thumping keyboards. Had I sought alternative opinions denigrating Aboriginal life and values and boosting the triumphs of the invaders, then judging from the copious flow of invective released by the High Court decision this book could have been filled in moments.

At first there was some pressure to include Aboriginal writers. I refused on the grounds that this book is an attempt to wrestle with Aboriginal Australia from the perspective of a later arrival.

Concern was also expressed about the title, though this speedily evaporated in discussions with Myrna Tonkinson (who wrote

Chapter 15). Even as a dot in the desert it is clear that Myrna is both a woman and black. Yet she has been labelled a whitefella, for the word is not to be taken too literally. It means an outsider, an alien, someone whose presence should generate caution, for whitefellas too often mean trouble.

In other words, the indigenous people of this country still regard the 16.8 million majority as most of us consider the police when they come uninvited, knocking on the door at unwelcome hours. What do they want? What's gone wrong? There's surely nothing good in it for me.

How come, after more than 200 years of living together, this distrust and apprehension and apartness remains? Is it a problem for the minority or the majority? The writers are clear on this one. It's an issue for us all.

There are nine men among the sixteen whitefellas who have so courageously exposed and shared their guilt, naivety, discoveries and joys. Seven of the authors were born overseas.

Teresa Ashforth, pregnant and alienated, looked through a train window, saw poverty she'd never encountered in Ireland and wondered why. She also listened to the language and recognised the cry of the conquered and oppressed. From this came a doctorate and a lasting commitment which included getting injured when police broke up a demonstration at Perth's old Swan Brewery where Aboriginal people and others were protesting against development on a sacred site.

(As is the way in Western Australia, their protests had little impact on the government [then Labor] which allowed the development to proceed.)

Ireland, and having an Irish ancestry, feature in the backgrounds of other contributors, as you'll discover. Perhaps because the Irish understand oppression, love the land and know what it's like to live on the fringe. Booker Prize winning author Roddy Doyle commented that the Irish are the blacks of Europe. A number of prominent Aboriginal people have also noticed the shared experience.

Kim Beazley also understands the Irish experience and its relationship with Aboriginal Australia. He knew the issues from an early age and spent twenty-three years in Federal Opposition urging change from the sidelines, a man decades ahead of his time. When he eventually achieved a ministry in the Whitlam Government, Kim drove himself to work eighteen hours a day in an attempt to make up the lost time. Now in retirement he recognises that oppression knows no racial boundaries. He also has a fine understanding of how the jigsaw of history fits together.

So does Geoffrey Bolton, now a senior academic at Edith Cowan University and an acknowledged expert on the shifts and shunts of our past. But when he started his academic career that past did not include Aboriginal history. As with so many, the world he knew as a young Australian was basically a transplanted Britain with a little black curiosity around the edges.

Catherine H Berndt brought her brilliant mind and Maori ancestry from Aotearoa to form one of the most remarkable and prolific partnerships in modern science. Despite being unable to walk, trapped in a hospital bed, a mountain of unfinished business before her and daily reminders of the loss of her husband, she was keen to discuss perceptions of colour and tell her story.

So was Ted Egan, whose outstanding commonsense approach to race relations is laced with a rugged appreciation of Aboriginal culture and celebration of our great good fortune in being able to share this continent. If only the granite-hearted economists, the conservative politicians with short-term goals, could embrace this talented man's humanity.

Victoria Laurie, represents hope for the future. Voraciously ambitious she studied in Japan, learned the language, joined the Australian Broadcasting Commision (ABC) and seemed destined for the executive suite. Instead she chose marriage and motherhood and created her own opportunities to write in depth on matters of substance. She welcomes the idea of a multi-cultural society where differences are celebrated, not feared. It is an Australia which is yet to be reflected in a media which still tends to seek answers from those driven by fear, not hope.

Bruce Petty starts this collection. His ability to distil the complex into one coarse line with a felt-pen has made him one of

Australia's greatest black-and-white artists. Added to that is his gentle humility and astonishingly inventive mind which has been applied in Chapter One, this time with words.

This book is full of insights. Diana Simmonds, who sees evils lurking in our suburbs similar to those she encountered in South Africa, offers a useful reminder. She tells us that Eddie Mabo, the man whose name heads the successful Murray Island claim to native title in the High Court, was only doing what Aboriginal people have long been urged to do by the white conservatives: assimilate; learn to read and write; get a job; do what we do. But when Aboriginal people turn to litigation, the lubricant which greases Australian commerce, that's not approved.

It's also a book of exploration. Every contributor has made his or her journey into the recesses of their soul where significant discoveries have been made. Fred Chaney, a Catholic who once, as a Liberal Minister for Aboriginal Affairs, had the key job in Australia with the chance to effect real change but found himself ranged against the powers of indifference, was about to abandon his assignment. Then he attended an Anglican Eucharist where Archbishop Desmond Tutu was preaching. And there were the right words for his essay. The key word is love.

Fred is a lawyer, a former politician and now an academic so he fills three categories of contributors. Five are from the universities, all in the social sciences and humanities. I look forward to future editions of this book when test-tube scientists, statisticians in bifocals and calculating economists can be recruited to comment on race relations. No doubt such issues worry the more staid professions, but so far they stay in the closet.

That's not been the position of Veronica Brady, probably Australia's best known nun and at times the social conscience of a nation. While other religious people satisfy their moral qualms by going on retreat, Dr Brady (who is also an academic) goes public, and often to her great cost. Her story in Chapter 12 recalled an event I witnessed as a reporter. When Sister Veronica had finished speaking out against the bigots in a suburban meeting (in a gentle, but persuasive style) she walked back up the aisle. Now it's important to note that, unlike so many male members of the clergy, this lady is no robust and portly person. In fact a good draught from a broken louvre could be a threat to her stability. As she walked away the ultimate ugly thong-clad Okker, pregnant with Swan Lager, stood up and deliberately jostled her progress.

There are four journalists among the writers. Others were invited, but shrank from the prospect, usually pleading a lack of time but, I fancy, really showing a reluctance to reveal. It's curious that this macho profession, so keen to pry into the lives of others, is shy when asked to look at itself. One story which escaped was told by a journalist from South Africa. On arriving at his new job with a major metropolitan paper he was invited by his colleagues for a drink. At the bar he expected to be questioned on life as a reporter in one of the world's hottest news spots. Or maybe the state of rugby football. Certainly there would be exchanges on the cost of living, salary scales, the best suburbs to select, and the way to find a good school or quality car. Instead he was given an ear-bashing of 'coon jokes'. We could all do with an analysis of that incident and the underlying reasons.

One answer is fear. That's an emotion identified by several contributors. The fear of the different, the unknown ... the fear of being found out. What better way to mask this primitive feeling than by cracking a joke in a pub. Or is it the problem of communicating in any depth, an irony for people who make their living in the communication industry.

There are two artists. Bruce Petty has already been mentioned; the other contributor is Robert Juniper, now discovering, like Catherine H Berndt, that he may not be 'pure' white after all, and quietly rejoicing at the discovery. However the admirers of his astonishing and original landscapes are apparently now taking a different view of his work. Racism in the salons of art? Surely discrimination is confined to pubs and workshops.

Robert Juniper's reaction to the likelihood of having Aboriginal ancestry returns us again to Aotearoa, where to have Maori blood is, in many cases, a matter of pride. It was in that country that the other lawyer who appears in this book, Hal

Jackson, discovered much about himself and Australia.

At the outset a judicial talkfest seems an unlikely event for a revelation. But the conference was opened by an eminent judge who asked the Maori elders present if it was okay to proceed. Can you imagine such an event in Australia? Hal Jackson could not, and his reaction to the experience helped make him the subject of a major noose-swinging public rally which persuaded the Labor Government to introduce legislation which affronted international agreements on child law. It's not easy being liberal.

Bill Bunbury is a social historian. In the style of the ABC where he works, this is a way of using two fancy words where one old-fashioned term would suffice. He is, of course, a storyteller and you can hear his tales most weeks on Radio National, though by the time you read this it will probably have another name. Like Hal Jackson, Bill Bunbury came late to Aboriginal Australia, but once there made it his business to learn more. And like so many of us, it was a small, seemingly inconsequential everyday event rather than a speech by a politician which swung him onto the path he now follows. A disabled car by the roadside. A couple looking for assistance. A chance comment by a relative and a new track appears which has to be followed, rough and tortuous though it seems.

Acclaimed Australian poet and author Judith Wright completes this collection. She is also a social historian, a fifth generation Australian who recognises that the prosperity of her family, or at least the male side, was built on stolen property. Her work in trying to improve understanding of our past and the need for a treaty has been outstanding.

As you read this book and encounter the anecdotes which have affected the writers maybe you'll wonder how you might handle such moments. You're in the middle of a dinner party with friends and relatives. Or maybe in the staff room at morning tea. Suddenly someone makes a racist remark or joke and almost everyone laughs. Do you object and get treated with derision, or risk getting involved in an angry debate where you're not well equipped? Or do you let the moment pass, rationalising that you made a telling look, or left the room and this would have had a mighty impact.

These events tend to ambush the unwary. You get in a cab and the driver apologises for being late. He explains that he's had to argue with a customer. 'You know what these blacks are like,' he says conspiratorially, certain you are on his side.

What do you do? Get out of the cab on some isolated road, express your indignation, threaten to report the conversation then hope an empty taxi will be cruising by and you won't be too late for that critical appointment? Or do you keep your mouth shut, substituting silence for action, arguing with your conscience that the driver would have been embarrassed by the mute non-compliance?

(After writing this a friend who had just returned from crewing a millionaire's yacht up the west coast told how meals became a litany of 'blackfella jokes'. His host, a major Western Australian businessman whose parents had been station lessees, told the crew he 'hated blacks'.)

If there's a common thread among the contributors it's that they're people who care and have persisted despite the pain. They are humans who ask questions and are seldom satisfied with the answers. They are adaptable, flexible people who have made discoveries, sometimes late, and have shifted the focus and direction of their lives to meet the new realities with courage and joy.

Which doesn't mean unquestioning acceptance of all things Aboriginal. There is a great mound of bullshit in this business. Not all Aboriginal people love their children, care for each other, treat the environment with care, respect the elders and have some mystical rapport with nature. That's because they're human beings, and like you and me subject to all the failings of the flesh.

Yet government departments continue to recruit Aboriginal people with minimal or no qualifications assuming that to be black is to have a deep appreciation of the culture and an innate ability to understand, communicate and interpret. Some do. Others don't. As Fred Chaney said during an ABC Radio National interview: 'The hardest thing for a white sympathiser is to criticise some Aboriginal responses and behaviour.' The charge of racism is easy to make and it hurts. As the pendulum slips away from overt racism, crass paternalism and moral superiority there are dangers it will move too far, taking on the unquestioning precious tone adopted by some broadcasters when they interview blacks.

Clearly the contributors in *Being Whitefella* are unlikely to make that mistake. They're intelligent, anxious, open-minded and humble human beings who treat others as equals and by so doing do not abandon their critical faculties. What finer set of writers would you want to meet?

They are also people who recognise the contradictions. Following the road of your conscience and concern means being tossed and bumped by the judder bars (as they're known across the Tasman) every time you gather pace. There are no simple answers, as Myrna Tonkinson shows so adequately. Being black doesn't necessarily mean affinity. Being whitefella is about behaviour.

And just when you think you might have got the hang of it all and the issues are starting to make sense, it all slips through your fingers and skids away, like soap in the shower.

Enough of the profound and puerile and the mixed metaphors. I also hope *Being Whitefella* will help demolish the Berlin Wall of suspicion and distrust erected by the most brutal of our predecessors, and reinforced by the closed minds of our contemporaries who believe the wealth of a society has to be measured in cash. If, through the frank observations and personal stories of the authors, this book helps you share the limitless mysteries of this land, to recognise the history great and mean, to forgive the wrongs and rejoice in the good fortune which has given us such beauty, bounty and common wealth, then another stage has been reached on the road to reconciliation.

And if all that sounds a bit ponderous, I hope you'll find *Being Whitefella* a good read and maybe a bit of a chuckle here and there. Race relations is serious stuff, but a wry smile at the insoluble, teasing mystery of it all can help now and again.

Duncan Graham

1

TRY LISTENING TO THE SOFTER VOICES

Bruce Petty

How do you draw a satirical cartoon about people you have been dispossessing for 200 years?

Technically, satire is about metaphors. So what's the right metaphor to use?

There are 270,000 Aboriginal people, and they've been here for 40,000 years, probably a lot more. There's 17 million of us and we've been here since 1788.

Now the metaphor search:

A large white dog irritated by a black flea?

No, that's not right.

Two different size animals fighting over territory?

Needs to be more epic.

A blot spreading on something abstract labelled conscience?

A ghost which keeps coming back to haunt? That's a bit closer.

Shakespeare is a good cartoon fallback.

A black ghost at a banquet: 'out damned spot', 'will these hands never be clean' – that's better.

Someone trying to unravel a knot of History...

We don't want to offend, we don't want to patronise. We don't want to give up the suburban block or the national park.

Assembling any sort of honest focus on Aboriginal issues, if you're white and middle-class, is a slippery process. One solution is not to. As well as champions of free speech in this country, we are very attached to the idea of free silence.

In the 1940s there was no problem with the Australian identity. We were friendly, brave, casual, fair go people with a sense of humour and a healthy disrespect for authority. National identity is largely self-assessment. We couldn't help noticing that we were white.

For Suburban Australians of my generation who were twenty-something in the 1950s, getting some sort of a perspective on anyone black was a chancy business.

The original Aboriginal stereotype we began with was constructed from Sunday school missionary stories, Joliffe cartoons, and sporting events. There was rarely a family to know or a black face to see.

All our information on 'coloured' races was indirect.

Othello was theatre.

The black African slave trade was history.

The Chinese threat was news.

Black tap dancers and musicians and waiters on American trains were show business.

Cosby was television.

All this was reinforced by the Ektacrome racial sterilising that occurred in the *National Geographic* in waiting rooms.

Nothing was experience.

None of our best friends were black.

The sum of it was the impression that coloured people were hard workers, happy, exotic, tough, musical, pagan, and lived in a good place to visit.

Coloured Races were a distant tourist photo opportunity.

There seemed to be a colour hierarchy. White had to be on top but you didn't go on about it. Then there were the Aborigines. Aborigines seemed to be an issue, not a people.

My lot, those white Australians who had their chance in the 1960s and 1970s, slowly, accidentally, assembled a rough kind of revision of this imagery.

Not so much a learning curve as an unlearning zig-zag.

A trip to England might include a stop-off in Bombay. The liveliness of streets full of brown human traffic in such disorder – the beggars seem inevitable. There seemed to be more laughing than you'd expect.

In Aden they glared at us.

We were being casual, fair go Australians with cameras. They must have mistaken us for someone else.

In the 1950s West Indians were migrating to live legally in Britain. Colour became an issue.

Enoch Powell made his 'rivers of blood' speech in the Commons. Disturbing race debates began.

In the 1950s and 1960s hundreds of remote coloured colonies became nations – where would they get the statesmanship? Black Ministers in some parliaments turned out to be Oxford dons, spoke upper-class English.

Some were upper-class parliamentary, English-speaking Marxists.

The neat order of things racial starts to slip away. Brown Indians began winning literature prizes in our language. Black Tanzanians were running faster than whites.

Black Nkrumah of Ghana being non-committed about communism raised a general alarm.

The cold war was simple enough: freedom versus dictatorship. But Russia, which is white, as well as being state controlled, seemed to be on the side of the coloured poor in the new nations. Our side, which is white and free, seemed to be on the side of the coloured rich.

So anyone for social justice had a fellow-travelling problem.

It was so worrying that Sociology courses took off. Weber, Durkheim and C Wright Mills.

Property is theft. The protestant ethic. The exploitation of Labour.

Marx gets referred to.

Western Capital and power in a few hands makes democracy a farce.

It needed an answer.

A J P Taylor said we doctor history.

There seemed to be a suggestion around that we might be, at times, the bullies of history.

With the Soviet Union invasion of Hungary, a lot of activists hurried off into peace movements.

Brown Egypt takes over the British-French canal.

What's happening to white power?

Mao tells nearly a billion light brown Chinese to let a thousand flowers bloom. It sounds better than white explanations for Hiroshima.

Light brown Vietnamese and carpet bombing suggested white military West was losing its judgment.

Had we got to the top by means of a lot of pre-television Vietnams?

The Colour issue gets enmeshed in: Peace, Nuclear Protest, Economic Strategy, the Third World, and Socialism.

Many White Australians discover the notion of simultaneous pride and self-criticism.

Canadian Red Indians are heard of. Tibetans. Laotians.

As Asia unfolded – so did the notion of white people being outnumbered.

The black civil rights movement in America rose up – articulate, violent and moving. The black panthers. Bussing.

Do it, said the sixties. The seventies began serious demonstrating. Tent cities outside Parliament.

The Chant of Jimmy Blacksmith by Thomas Keneally.

The Savage Crows by Robert Drewe.

My generation of White Australians finally had to take notice. Aborigines seemed to fit a picture of misallocation of power and wealth.

As the seventies were roughly about the family of man as well as oil, some legislation connecting the two cultures was passed.

Deaths in Custody was a reminder of how little actually connected. Now Mabo, and the High Court attempts to connect the two property systems. White Australia is more and more pressured to decide what it thinks about Aboriginies.

Random personal images add to this sequence:

The insolent sprawl of sharp African American blacks riding the New York underground.

Listening to blues singer John Lee Hooker in a tiny, sweaty, upper-floor room.

A discussion about thick black African lips and white thin lips.

A discussion with a Queensland urban Aborigine about my method of caricaturing Aborigines.

Filming a young Vietnamese being captured by marines in the rice paddies.

A black township beer hall in Rhodesia.

Michael Long playing Aussie Rules.

A busload of white tourists disembarking in Delhi and looking very peculiar.

Pat O'Shane angry.

Ernie Dingo funny.

An Aborigine called Banjo on a cattle station outside Normanton wanting to ask the manager a question. He appeared on his haunches in the grass looking into the distance, beyond the sprinklers watering the lawn in front of the verandah where the manager was having a beer. Banjo reappeared 20 metres to the right in the grass, slightly closer, looking at the ground. Three more silent moves. The manager called out to him and they talked.

Black Aborigines working cattle, shooting and skinning a steer.

That is maybe a kind of average race input list my generation of media people is likely to assemble. It represents a long, erratic, partial sensitising of a particular generation of white Australia to the Aboriginal issue.

The response to it varies, it seems, from nagging guilt to sympathetic indifference.

A few points:

One:

Hardly any of the sensitising came from the education system.

Cultural interchange may not be enough.

Aboriginal studies in schools might not do it.

A more honest history might help.

A more honest account of the origins and morality of white Western dominance might be a start.

Two:

You get the feeling the 1970s was the end of 100 years of

erratic pursuit of social justice.

The 1980s was a huge misallocation of wealth.

The 1990s is about keeping it that way. Bad luck, black Australia.

The 1993 Native title legislation was just Australia coming in late.

Three:

The useful messages will come from the fringe of power. The great professional noise of experts has to play the media sound-bite game.

We must get better at listening to softer voices.

We have expected all our wisdom to come from clever exchanges, sophisticated, orderly, forceful confrontational minds.

We have a legal process that operates so.

It seems to me the best shifts in attitude are the result of none of these characteristics.

Alternative social priorities and awkward history, and religious, and cultural views held deeply by Aborigines will never match our smart, media-driven voices of aggressive conservatism. Either they get noisy or we get gentle.

Perhaps reflective, imaginative, untidy thinking is at the beginning of solutions to problems – then the noise.

Part of the answer is honest history.

My lot were lied to. Then we lied to one another. Then we got used to lies. Now we need them. We must stop doing it.

This Cartoon problem though ...

– this white person trying to eat a big dinner while banging his/her head with a big hammer labelled guilt and ...

– a white Australian racing around in a spiral labelled history with a large chain attached to ...

– a white toilet with...

It's too hard.

37

2

DIFFERENT WAYS OF TALKING

Teresa Ashforth

As an Irish woman brought up on a diet of Irish history written by Irish scholars, I found it comparatively easy to identify with the concept of cultural colonialism. This has been as central to the conquest of Aboriginal Australia as it was to the much earlier conquest of Ireland by the English.

Definitions of culture are as diverse as there are ways of speaking about the idea. It depends upon your discipline, orientation and point of view, but it can't be denied that language in all its forms is critical to any culture. Language constitutes the central dynamic of any race. It establishes a nation's sense of itself, its identity and destiny.

As a reluctant migrant to Australia in the late 1960s, accompanying my English husband and six of what were later to become our eight children (two were born here), I came to a country at once strange and yet familiar.

It was strange because the country often described as 'young' immediately belied that label. To me the hot dry sands and burnt-out earth, the old and sad grey trees standing dead in parched paddocks mocked by rusty windmills and dusty tracks, all these markers in the landscape were a source of added torment to the bleak sense of total loss in double exile which was my bitter experience at that time. My jaundiced eyes could see nothing to compensate for what I'd left behind either in Ireland or indeed in the England and London I'd also learned to love.

Time passes and we change. I grew to love Australia as my

home, to appreciate the uniquely different beauty of its landscapes, and, most of all, the friends I made. But right from the start, from the first train ride into Perth from the foothills, I felt an additional unease. At the time I was unable to explain this emotion to myself or to my daughters who were with me.

In those days we passed through an East Perth very different from the present suburb. From the train it was possible to see, indeed impossible to miss, groups of Aboriginal people living on the then 'fringes' of an earlier and less cosmopolitan city.

My eldest daughter was nine and had never seen images of such poverty in her life. When I told her they were Aboriginal people, the original inhabitants and owners of Australia before white people came, she was puzzled and said: 'Can't we do something to help them?' Preoccupied as I then was with the impending arrival of our first-born Australian, all I could do was applaud her concern and agree that we should indeed 'do something'.

Yet many years passed before I had the privilege of meeting Aboriginal people for the first time. My thoughts often reverted to my daughter's concern with a very real sense of personal guilt when we could see to the right of the old road approaching Midland Junction the miserable and inadequate shelters of the fringe-dwellers of the Swan Valley.

The Fringedwellers, when I came to know them, described how they were constantly moved by the police from their illegal camps and resting places. Then they had to find, as best they could, alternative and equally temporary places to stay. (In a neat twist the Swan Valley Fringedwellers much later took the dismissive term, capitalised the word and registered an Association.)

As immigrants we shared in the general amnesia of that earlier time. We succeeded in persuading ourselves that our imagined white community constituted the 'real' Australia. Our generous gesture of affirmation in response to the referendum of 1967 (which approved a change in the Federal Constitution to allow Aborigines to be treated as Australians in matters like census taking, and to allow the Federal government predominance in

Aboriginal policy), and which at one level persuaded us that we were doing a good thing, completely failed to evoke any awareness of the irony implicit in this act of largesse.

Talk of a referendum regarding the Mabo legislation eerily echoes those even less enlightened days when we suppressed our concerns for the rightful inheritors of the land we so unthinkingly enjoy.

After the disruption of the relationship between white settlers and their Aboriginal retainers who were no longer to be a source of cheap or free labour (in 1965 the Commonwealth Conciliation and Arbitration Commission established normal award rates for Northern Territory Aboriginal stockmen), I was assured by my liberal Australian-born friends that 'things' used to be 'very much better' when Aboriginal people, together with their families, were 'well looked after' by the station owners and were really happy and friendly people 'in those days'. They conveniently forgot, if they ever knew, the full impact such 'looking after' had on the lives of the people concerned. This was something I also had to learn.

Not from the media however. Then, as now (though with some significant and distinguished exceptions), the media seemed to see preservation of our somewhat self-righteous comfort zone as the first priority. The press, radio and television continued to justify the unjustifiable, treating Aboriginal people both as the 'lesser' and as 'the other'. This longstanding tradition of Eurocentric and imperialistic representation, based on a similar anthropology and ethnography, is only now being seriously and effectively challenged. Its legacy is deeply rooted in our national psyche. It will require a good deal more than a few white-run social justice 'task forces' if we are to succeed in altering our consciousness and attitudes.

Studies of the representation of indigenous people in the mainstream media have shown an unacceptable degree of negative bias and Aboriginal under-representation. Although some strong and powerful Aboriginal voices are at last being foregrounded in the Aboriginal media and public forums, it is still far too unequal a contest in terms of the representation of their legitimate views.

Nowhere has this been more evident than with the historic Mabo decision. This runs a very real risk of being perverted by concerns for our exclusive interests. Perhaps we should know better at a time when our consciences are preoccupied with thoughts of reconciliation.

True reconciliation is unlikely to be brought about by legislation alone, rather by attention to a host of cultural considerations of which language is one of the foremost. I was sufficiently convinced of this to study and research to clarify for myself, and hopefully for others, some of the questionable aspects of communication between Aboriginal people, police and lawyers. The genesis for this work lay in those early days of my arrival in Australia.

We lived in the hills not far from the fertile Swan Valley, famous now for its rich vineyards. Pleasure boats regularly take tourists up the river to taste the wines and enjoy the good food of the elegant restaurants along the way. Less well known and seldom touted as an exotic attraction is the fact that the Swan Valley Fringedwellers can trace their unbroken occupancy of the valley for 40,000 years or more.

Their rituals and modern-day corroborees are less colourful and audience-friendly now than they might have been in earlier days, for the culture is more diversified. The people are preoccupied with survival in a still sometimes hostile and condescending social climate. Their immediate concerns are finding bearable accommodation, feeding and educating the children, staying out of gaol, protecting their youth from substance abuse and other contemporary hazards, and, far too often, in burying their dead.

Happy revellers returning to Perth along the Swan River in the light of the setting sun can hardly be expected to be conscious of the oppressed yet vibrant and dynamic subculture through whose unacknowledged territory they pass.

Noongars have over the years been joined by other Aboriginal people from outside their territory. At first it was the need for grape-pickers. Later people became more mobile. Many were displaced from their homelands by the ill-advised social engineering of the times, or for the economic benefit of non-Aboriginal people and the convenience of the government.

Some housing experiments which group disparate Aboriginal people into one area have failed to take sufficient account of territorial and clan sensitivities. Several have been disastrously unsuccessful and have contributed to a debilitating anomie amongst a basically proud, dignified and spiritual people.

In the late 1970s I was lucky enough to meet Margaret Jeffery, a psychologist and now my long-term friend. Unlike myself, Margaret had years earlier discovered ways to be of assistance to Aboriginal people. She lived in Guildford where their plight was particularly evident. Margaret found a practical approach. This eventually became a way of life in which she succeeded without fear or favour in joining Aboriginal people in their ongoing and wearying search for justice.

As a result of my friendship with Margaret, and when most of my children had become adults, I was able to meet the people who succeeded in making me feel truly 'at home' in Australia. That's what I meant when I spoke earlier of this country's capacity to make me feel that it was in some way strange, and in other ways familiar.

But without Margaret's mediating and instructive role it would not have been so easy for me to become accepted. I owe her a great deal. She was there before me and continues to play an active role of unstinting service. I'll follow her excellent example where she takes down and re-presents the words of the Aboriginal people for whom she works, unedited and accurate, without altering either the meaning or the content. I'll let her words speak:

> *I grew up with a strong sense of justice and fairness. I came to Australia at 11 years old expecting to encounter Aboriginal people, but all I saw were people disappearing in the shadows.*
>
> *As a kid I unconsciously learnt the Australian denial, no*

acknowledgment or speaking about the people of the land: 'out of sight, out of mind'. It took being in England in the sixties to see from afar that the fundamental issue for Australia was the human rights of the indigenous people.

Then suddenly in the seventies everyone white had an opinion, but never dreamt of actually engaging with, or listening to Aboriginal people. Colonialism continued.

I was the same as everyone else – ignorant and opinionated. Did no one imagine how Aboriginal people felt and feel now at all these jumped-up and instant experts on Aboriginal issues? As I later saw, through Aboriginal eyes, we in our culture have given up the 'sovereignty of the person' in making decisions and taking actions for ourselves on things of importance (outside of mostly small personal and material concerns). We talked a lot but kept living the way we lived. We changed nothing in our actions or our lifestyle to take cognisance of Aboriginal human rights and concerns.

But one white man had an ear for the off-beat, and, like Ghandi, attended to 'the other', the exception, the dissident, the unheard voice, and I began reading his reports in the Daily News. *I read of a brave little band of Aboriginal people in the Swan Valley who were trying to do something to help themselves; who were speaking for themselves; who had stopped running and saying 'yes'.*

It was journalist Jim Magnus who I later found was celebrated in the Aboriginal community because he went out day or night to find Aboriginal people to hear their side of the story so he could report it, however unpopular or challenging. Of course editors were unsympathetic. Who wanted to hear the other side? Most Australians fail to understand this: that nearly all that they see in the media concerning Aboriginal issues is without the real Aboriginal (grassroots) voice, the other side of the story.

We're not talking about people who say what the government wants to hear. Jim Magnus never took the received opinion, the view of the authorities, the assimilation position with-

out question. He knew there were two cultures, two laws, two perspectives, two languages, two sides of the story. He is loved by Aboriginal people for recognising and reporting that. He was to endure criticism, reprimands and even threats of dismissal for his principled stand. He will be remembered for this.

Jim brought me in, and then it was Aboriginal people who re-educated me – Robert Bropho and his brothers and sisters and mother, and Edna Bropho; George Pickett, Louis Nettle, Matthew Anderson, Minnie Harris and many others, brave and courageous and inspiring people, many of whom have since, sadly, passed away.

My re-education really happened on the 'Journey of the Forgotten People to Parliament House, Canberra' in 1977. (See Robert Bropho's book Fringedweller.*) Living, eating, sleeping, travelling, going to hospitals, going to Aboriginal camps on the way across for three weeks, with the forty Fringedwellers from the Swan Valley who crossed the continent for their cause in spite of hardship and constant and extreme suffering. The experience opened my eyes and mind. Racism and oppression and discrimination and prejudice every single day in every aspect of life. I realised most white people have no idea what Aboriginal people face on a daily basis. That is still so today.*

I found humanity, that everyone is important and to be taken seriously. No hierarchy here, high or low. I found tolerance and acceptance of people however eccentric or 'unrespectable'. I found white hypocrisy and prejudice. I saw people bravely speaking the unacceptable truth and not being cautious or making deals or looking for a spin-off. I found care and sociability with the old, the weak, the sick, and the alcoholic. I found wonderful communal child care. I found sharing, and forgiveness of white oppression, and learned that hatred gets you nowhere.

And I found what is called 'political' in blacks is not political: it is religious. And I found that this non-material value system is mostly completely misunderstood and ignored and yet would, I believe, hugely benefit our society. Richard Leakey, who wrote Making of Mankind, *says those hunter-gatherer values have served humankind for 100,000 years of survival. And yet our society is still seeking assimilation to our values. The recommendations and actions of the Royal Commission into Aboriginal Deaths in Custody are nearly all assimilationist in character.*

Of course all this led to a shaking up and remaking of my life. For a time I would have endless arguments with my friends and some relatives. Then I stopped arguing and realised the only way for whites is to communicate openly and directly with Aboriginal people. Then away goes the fear and the guilt and antagonism.

From there can we make the next step and recognise our people as invaders and begin to meet the human rights of Aboriginal people?

Knowing Margaret and the Fringedwellers helped refine my ear. Slowly the view from the window of a speeding train was replaced by more personal contact. I started to listen to the people and their language. I wanted to know more.

My preoccupation with language led me to explore the different ways of speaking which can cause and perpetuate many undesirable aspects of our relationships with each other. I suspected that Aboriginal people, especially in their relationship with white law, might be particularly disadvantaged because of the way they speak.

My first task was to discuss this with the Aboriginal people I knew, and seek their assistance. Their encouragement, support and help, while it came as no surprise, nevertheless was both central and crucial to the task.

Through Robert Bropho I came to know and appreciate many of his family members and extensive kin, particularly his late mother. For me, to have become known, and to be introduced to strangers, as 'Granny's friend', was both an honour and a guarantee of my bona fides as an acceptable and unremarkable 'Wadjila' woman in their midst.

Sadly, amongst the far too many premature Aboriginal deaths which have occurred in that particular community over the period since they became my friends have been three of Granny's adult sons and two of her daughters – a reflection on the intolerably greater mortality rate amongst the underprivileged in a land of comparative prosperity.

The funerals were to educate me further into the strength, care and cohesion of Aboriginal society. Relatives and friends from throughout the State and across the continent from Darwin, Adelaide and other eastern cities joined to give dignified support to mourners for the loss of one of their own in a uniquely Aboriginal way. I have been privileged to have joined them on far too many occasions.

The familiarity I felt with Aboriginal people in spite of our different skin colour and histories didn't just arise from the fact that their way of speaking English wasn't 'mainstream' and standard. Important aspects of their lives and the things they discussed were also different. It reminded me of Irish country people who speak what some scholars refer to as a 'hybrid' form of English. They've lost their native tongue, but the language they use still owes much to that root stock and bears the traces of its original characteristics. It can also construct a different set of experiences.

In a society which endorses 'Standard English' as the most acceptable way of communicating, the fact that the Noongars (and Aboriginal people in other parts of Australia born into an English-speaking environment) have their own distinctive dialect seems of little account.

The universal currency of 'Standard English' and its grammar has plenty of advantages. Competence is shared globally by a large number and wide variety of peoples and nationalities. However, underpinning this competence is a tendency towards the insidious idea that other languages or dialects are somehow inherently impoverished, deficient, or 'lack grammar'.

One of the most socially and philosophically valuable contributions made by modern linguistics is to challenge and make specious such ideas. Linguistic studies now recognise and validate the claim that a characteristic form of talking within a specific speech community has its own rules of grammar. It contains its own separate registers of use, and it carries a set of rules regarding appropriate speech behaviour according to situation and context.

I don't want to generalise about this because many Aboriginal people have long ago mastered Standard English and are both bi-dialectal, well educated in 'Western' terms as well as in their own, and are particularly articulate. Nevertheless there are still many people who have suffered because they haven't been properly understood, or have been talked-down by the people who have had most power over them, either through institutional authority or as a result of conflict-laden encounters.

The important thing about language is that dissimilar groups use language differently. While these patterns of usage are related to each other, they are not the same. They can be the site of contest, struggle, and ambiguity. While experience of such ambiguities and misunderstandings are common to us all, they are often magnified when it comes to intercultural communication.

We have to remember that talking, as well as 'saying' something to someone, is always, and at the same time, 'doing' something to someone. It's here that the question of language in relation to power and domination is so important. It's crucial in different contexts, at different sites, and at different levels.

Among the many forms of official or institutional ways of communicating, legal ways of communicating, for example, possess some special distinguishing characteristics. These contribute to making it accepted and legitimate.

These characteristics are enshrined both in the ritual trappings of the law and in the elitist character of the people who practise law. But above all they are active in the process where ordinary language and meanings can be translated and transformed into the closed and specialised code of the legal system under the guise of conventional practices of speaking and writing.

Lawyers, the jobs they do and the places where they work represent at one level a platform of mediation between condemnation and reprieve for the individual accused of breaking the law. However the accused person is usually in a vulnerable position which may well be disguised by the seemingly natural order of the language processes which are involved.

For cultural and sociological reasons such vulnerability is intensified when the lawyer's client is an Aboriginal person. Some lawyers are sensitive to such vulnerability and take it into account in their relations with Aboriginal people. However the fact remains that in the course of their training to become professionals, they have become part of a discourse which often puts them at a distance from their clients.

Over and above the immediate responsibility for representing Aboriginal clients in individual cases, lawyers (perhaps more than they realise) are also in a position where they represent 'white' discourse in an intercultural context.

The institutional discourse of the law is, of course, only one of many such discourses. You'll find others in education, science, medicine, psychiatry and the military. It's the way language is used where one culture can be effectively colonised and dominated by another (at least until such time as the oppressed can master these same discourses). Paulo Freire in his book *Pedagogy of the Oppressed* explored the resistance to this aspect of language-as-power most effectively in the context of Latin America.

Colonisers and missionaries alike can sometimes be excused on the grounds of ignorance for many of the injustices visited on the colonised. While some missionaries take the trouble to document and preserve the languages, and protect the culture of the spiritually colonised, it wasn't so much ignorance but deliberate policy which motivated the secular colonisers. They tried to impose their own languages and extinguish those of the conquered. They did this in Ireland and Australia with comparable success. I was conscious of some similarities.

My studies and research confirmed that white law can disadvantage Aboriginal people in particular. Problems arise not only because of differences in many 'Western' and Aboriginal world views, but also from the greater importance given to the written over the spoken word in that regular chain of discourse in which Aboriginal people accused of breaking the law become involved.

In most cases this difference does much to aggravate the continuing gulf between us. Addressing it might go some way towards righting ancient and ongoing wrongs and could pave the way for a form of reconciliation between our hybrid selves.

And yet in our ever-changing world exceptions abound. Films like *Exile and the Kingdom*, *Blackfellas*, books like Anna Haebich's *For Their Own Good* and Duncan Graham's *Dying Inside* and a growing number of films, books, plays and music by Aboriginal people, as well as Royal Commissions and reform movements, all play their part in awakening the sleeping consciences of all Australians.

Despite some still lively racism in this country, I'm constantly encouraged by the raised consciousness of the many students I have known, both Aboriginal and non-Aboriginal, who take very seriously this aspect of our lives together. Hopefully they will one day make Australia a better and more just place, if only they are encouraged and permitted to do so.

3

TOO MANY MINGY BUGGERS

Fred Chaney

Australia fits me like an old shoe. On the infrequent occasions I leave, I become restless about returning. Flying back is always one of the best moments of a trip away. The first glimpse of shoreline from the plane window brings a thrill of pleasure. The only television advertisement I positively enjoyed was the Qantas commercial to the theme 'I still call Australia home'. It reminded me of how I feel coming home.

My work has taken me to every corner of the place. Camping in Arnhem Land or on Cape York seems no more foreign than Rottnest, beloved since childhood, or Margaret River which I now see as partly my country.

That is why the secession talk which bubbles up from time to time in Western Australia I find offensive. Why would I want to cut off from people throughout Australia who never seem foreigners to me and from places which are mine?

There are of course lots of things about Australia to arouse discomfort. Take your choice according to your interests. I am uneasy about the drift away from fair distribution of income, the breakdown of intergenerational equity as those with young dependants are increasingly penalised.

Horrifyingly, neglect and brutalisation of children seem to be on the increase, an even more important issue than the loss of plant and animal species, which seems to attract more concern. But overall this is a good country, a good place to be and to come home to.

But I know it isn't like that for everyone. It isn't for the brutalised child, or for the long-term unemployed, or for some struggling families. It is the truth for some that they are excluded in one way or another from the snugness – even perhaps the smugness – of my Australia.

The most puzzling part for me is the response to Aboriginal Australia and the way we have so often treated Aborigines as foreigners. It seems that the response on all sides is visceral or instinctive, rather than intellectual. Talking with a pro-Aboriginal woman and expressing some doubts about a particular Aboriginal position, I am confronted by a denial of the relevance of the facts. To this person it is not the facts which count but the importance of solidarity with the beleaguered group.

On the other side of the debate there is deep resentment at perceived Aboriginal advantage. Often Aboriginal people seem to be regarded as sub-human, not warranting the respect given other human beings. The notion of their having rights acknowledged by the law is an affront to the sense of order.

In a bizarre paradox, Aboriginal people manage to be in trouble with their fellow Australians for being disadvantaged and privileged at the same time.

I guess that's the thing I have felt uncomfortable about most often. The rank injustice, the unfairness, that is the lot of so many Aboriginal Australians. Not for them the land of the fair go, outsiders in their own country.

So I am puzzled about my country in this respect.

How is it that we have managed to turn so many Aboriginal Australians into foreigners in their own country?

Not all, of course. Thousands of Aboriginal Australians are confident members of the community on their terms.

The range is impressive. We have just lost Oodgeroo Noonuccal, but Jack Davis, Sally Morgan and many others write. Ernie Dingo acts and dances. Stumpy Brown/Nyugu and her five fellow female painters from Fitzroy Crossing join with better known artists like Rover Thomas and many others in producing new schools in the visual arts.

Polly Farmer, Michael Long, Evonne Goolagong, Charles Perkins, Galarrwuy Yunupingu, Gatjil Djerrkura, Wesley Lanapuy, in sport, administration, politics, business, the heroes are there, along with thousands of quiet achievers.

But underneath the layers of success and well-being are even greater numbers who fit uncomfortably into our view of our country and ourselves. Those awful statistics highlighted in the Borrie Report on Population in 1973, about Aboriginal health, education, employment, life expectancy and so on, have become a litany of reproach. We know too much is wrong, sometimes we are sorry about it, sometimes we resent it, 'After all we've done ...'

It is a long time since I thought Aboriginal Australia was the childhood delight of the Durack sisters' *The Way of the Whirlwind.* It is a long time since my father's wartime story of his trip across the Nullarbor in a railway cattle truck and his contact with the man begging for a cigarette was part of our innocence.

'You mingy bugger' was my father's thanks for the handing over of his last couple of cigarettes to an Aboriginal man who'd asked for a smoke. It became part of our family's vernacular. Any act that was less than generous brought forth 'oo mingy bugger'. We didn't stop to think we might have been mingy buggers on a grander scale.

I remember the end of my innocence as a series of incidents from mid-teens through to the present day. The notion of outcast, that someone wasn't of sufficient value to be included, that someone didn't fit, I learned by personal parable. The notion that something wasn't right was drawn from experience, not from history.

On a holiday visit to a friend's farm was the first actual meeting with a different reality. I was staying with a large, close, cheerful family like my own. The country setting was different and so was the fact that they had an Aboriginal maid. She seemed a pleasant, obliging girl, though not as cheerful as the rest of us. She was there, but she wasn't part of it. I couldn't work it out. She just wasn't part of the world I knew and enjoyed.

Later that year I asked my friend at school about the remembered, isolated girl. He was dismissive. 'She's like the rest, gone off and got herself pregnant.'

I remember that clearly because, as a rather prudish schoolboy, I was surprised at how I felt. I thought she could not be blamed for taking any offer of affection, living as she did in isolation.

It didn't make sense. Why did outgoing, loving people draw the line at her?

A few years later during vacation employment, just seventeen and still prudish, I shared a bush hut on a grain siding with a roofing gang. They were rough and tough. Returning to the hut a bit tiddly from dinner at a nearby farm, I found my way in the dark to my bed, which was crowded in with five others. Lying in bed, I lit a cigarette and heard a female voice ask me for a cigarette. I lit a match and found myself facing an element of Aboriginal-white relations for which I wasn't prepared. I fled. I thought these women were really copping it hard. Despised during the day, used at night.

During my student days and then as a young lawyer, what I saw was a consistent pattern that didn't make sense. No right to vote, no right to be counted, miserable living conditions, family dismemberment, false accusations, unjust imprisonment. None of this is ancient history; it is just what I saw and experienced.

My sense of Aboriginal Australia isn't a matter of guilt about the past. It is just that the present I witnessed, and still see too often, didn't make any sense in terms of the way we in Australia generally see and treat each other.

Perhaps one more negative anecdote will do.

In my first years of law practice I was known to have an interest in Aboriginal people and issues. One day I had a call from an articled clerk in an adjacent firm, who told me he had a problem and asked me to see him. He came to my office and told me he was in a very embarrassing position, having taken instructions from an Aboriginal woman to defend a case being brought against her by the welfare authorities.

They were seeking to have her children declared neglected. If the case succeeded, her six children would be institutionalised. He said that she had paid him money on account of costs and he thought she had a good case, but he had been told by his principals that they did not act for Aborigines. He asked me if I would take the case on. I agreed.

The woman he brought to see me was, to my young eyes, middle-aged. She told me she had six children in a common law marriage, but her husband was currently in prison. I asked her about the children, all of whom were school aged, and she spoke convincingly of how well cared for they were.

I thought I would need supporting evidence and in turn rang the headmaster of the school the children attended, her landlord, the local store, the Salvation Army and an Aboriginal woman who worked in a government department as a cleaner and knew the family well.

It was an unusual set of calls, because all the people I rang were happy to go to court on her behalf. As any lawyer would know, that is not the common pattern. The headmaster confirmed the children were regular attenders, well behaved and appeared well looked after. The landlord confirmed she was a good tenant, who paid her rent on time and looked after the old and run-down house well. The Salvation Army officer said she knew the family and regarded the mother as a very good parent who cared for her children. The corner store knew my client as a customer with a credit account which was paid regularly. The Aboriginal woman described the family as close and the children given good care.

In court there seemed to be much confusion. When I indicated that the matter was contested, the public servant bringing the complaint proceeded to read out evidence from the bar table. He seemed rather surprised when I suggested that if there was to be any evidence, it had to be given on oath. Eventually he was sworn in and gave what can only be described as very thin evidence of any neglect of the six children. My witnesses were duly called and gave their evidence as they had explained the position to me and of course the case was dismissed.

I was young then, one eighth Irish and in a fair sort of rage by the time the case was over. Outside the court I berated the public servant who had brought it. He made two statements I found significant. The first was that it was the only such case he had known to have been defended, and the second was his response to my question as to why he had brought this complaint against a respectable woman who appeared to be a good mother to her children. His explanation was that the department had received complaints about too many Aborigines in East Perth, so 'welfare' was moving them out.

I should stress I'm not telling some story of ancient and forgotten times. I'm talking about the 1960s. I'm talking about the time when Sally Morgan's mother told her children they were Indian. Who could be surprised at people wishing to hide their Aboriginality when such cruel and inhumane treatment could be meted out to them in the name of welfare.

In this case, the reaction by government officials to satisfy a public demand for fewer Aborigines in East Perth was to seek the institutionalising of six children, taking them away from a caring mother.

There is, incidentally, a quite touching sequel to this story which does not particularly fit my narrative, but let me tell it anyway.

A few years ago I read of the complaints of the children of an Aboriginal woman who had died of a heart attack. The complaint was that the ambulance had been slow in coming and perhaps if it had been more timely then their mother might have survived. I recognised the name and checked, and sure enough it was my old client. I thought it was a nice repayment of her determination to fight for her children that the children were fighting for her even after her death, a quarter of a century after she had fought for them.

The point of these anecdotes is to explain my view that Aboriginal disadvantage is not a matter of ancient history.

For the whole of my adult life I have been repeatedly surprised by the evidence of harsh attitudes and behaviour towards those Australians who maintain their Aboriginality. Typical during the early 1990s has been the fallout from the Mabo judgment, which has changed from a hope of better times to a debate calculated to worsen race relations.

There seems to be widespread resentment about the fact that the Mabo judgment means that for a small number of Aboriginal people at least, that relatively small minority who have been able to maintain actual physical connection with land and the cultural web which binds them to that land, there is to be a qualitatively different future. In the past Aborigines have been moved on whenever they were in the way, with no regard for their social or economic interests. We have shown no more concern than if they were a mob of grazing kangaroos.

Sometimes I wonder if I have developed too negative a view. When I hear someone distinguished, learned and decent, Dame Leonie Kramer, in the 1993 Menzies Oration caution against too negative a view of our history and remind us of the instruction given to Governor Phillip to pay proper regard to the interests of the Aboriginal people, of his restraint even in the face of injury to himself and of wrongs which were wrought by both sides of the settlement equation, I have moments of doubt.

But then I am reminded of the consistency of my experience with our history by others like the Western Australian historian Pat Jacobs. In her book *Mr Neville*, an account of the life of Auber Octavius Neville, the Chief Protector of Aborigines from 1915 to 1940, she gives a careful account of Aboriginal policies and administration in Western Australia in the generation before I was born.

The book charts the callous indifference of most of the community, the sub-human treatment of Aborigines in the north and the south of Western Australia. This included trucking off the unwanted fringe-dwellers to camps in no way equipped to provide educational employment and social opportunities. This is the historic base from which the experiences I recount flow. Unhappily I find an unbroken thread running through her account of the past and the living experiences of my generation.

Almost daily I am reminded by some comment or argument of the resentment which exists at anything less than full assimilation of the Aborigines into our society. What is successful, what is acceptable, is measured strictly in our terms. It is hard to find support for a reasonable liberal view that we want an integrated society which admits people who are entitled to be different.

It is not uncommon to hear in discussion, or even to read in the letters page in newspapers, that Aborigines should be grateful for the fact that we rescued them from their miserable lives. Yet some historians say that the Aborigines were better nourished than the people of Europe at the time of settlement.

I have no way of making a personal judgment on that historic fact, but photographs taken by the first academic anthropologist in Australia, Baldwin Spencer, between 1894 and 1927 repay study. The photographs show tribal people in some of the harshest and remotest parts of Australia.

What is striking is the physical condition of men, women and children alike, their strength, their grace and their beauty. Men in the shape of warriors, women of beauty and cherubic children.

As I write this and look at the photograph of about thirty Aranda men in fighting mode, I am reminded of sitting with old men under a high neon light at Ti Tree Station in the Northern Territory and being struck by their dignity and strength, as well as the beauty of the scene; of sitting on a blue groundsheet south of Aurukan on Cape York in brilliant moonlight, while old men sang me the songs of their country. I feel sad that we cannot all enjoy what they are and what they can bring to us.

There are terrible dilemmas in every location where there is a displaced Aboriginal population. The people are forever changed and changing as their society responds to overwhelming numbers and the wonders of our technology. There can be no realistic proposal to return to the past. Aboriginal people will want the advantages of modern life, just as they wish to retain some of the valuable elements of their culture which are deeply ingrained in them.

Of course, the Aboriginal people in the circumstances I have mentioned will withstand the changes as best they can to maintain their identity, their sense of community and their belief in the value of their own society. I am sure they will be a continuing and often different presence in Australia.

Our superior attitudes, our lack of regard, our preparedness to be harsh and to ignore their rights as human beings when it suits our convenience, make it much harder than it should be.

There is nothing in our past or our present which suggests it is safe for Aborigines to rely on our consistency or our favour. One lesson Aborigines have taught me about being whitefella, indeed about being human, is that it is not safe to let anyone have too much power over other people. It just isn't safe.

At the end of writing this down I kept asking what it was I was trying to say. I discussed it at length with my wife and we concluded that the point of the story was that things could be better if we all just tried harder and behaved better.

Well, after the deadline for submitting the copy and still wrestling with what I was trying to say, we went to an Anglican Mass in St George's Cathedral to hear Archbishop Desmond Tutu preach. Towards the end of the service there was a last sentence of scripture – new to me :

> The Lord has showed you what is good; and what does the Lord require of you but to do justice, and to love kindness, and to walk humbly with God? (Micah 6:8)

We turned to each other with the common recognition that it sums up much of what our experiences suggest is required. This is a great country, but it could do with more justice, more kindness and more humility when we deal with the Aboriginal people we have made foreigners in their land.

In our land.

4

CRY FOR THE LOST CHANCES

Victoria Laurie

On an overcast day, winged harbingers of rain dot the grey Fremantle skies. The white-tailed black cockatoos cry plaintively 'wee-lah, wee-lah' as they glide across the sprawl of urban settlement. They appear near the coast each autumn, travelling birds on their way to diminishing nesting sites in the wheatbelt.

From the moment I settled into suburban life in the west, the black cockatoos' seasonal appearance captivated me. I felt compelled to run outside and watch them alight on the branches of a lemon-scented gum, a solitary wild giant in our street of neat houses. Clumsy and argumentative in repose, the heavy birds would as suddenly launch into graceful flight, wheeling over backyards and uttering cries like world-weary critics.

Someone told me the Aboriginal people around Perth called these cockatoos 'oo-lack' after their call. In the Albany region, they called them 'woo-lock'; around the Avon River there were two names for these birds and at the Pallinup River, another name again. Yet non-Aboriginal people, I soon discovered, barely had a name for them. 'Oh, those black cockies,' they'd say, 'tell you the truth, I've never much noticed them', even as the air filled with 'wee-lah, wee-lah' and the sky darkened momentarily as the flock passed overhead. 'They bring the rain,' my old neighbour offered.

Calyptorhynchus funereus latirostris, or Carnaby's Cockatoo are the little-known European names for the bird that, unaccountably, has come to have a strange effect on me. Their appearance, their 'wee-lah' cry, invokes a momentary sense of loss, as if reminding me of the failure of non-Aboriginal Australians to 'connect' with the plants, animals, contours and hidden spirits of our own country.

The black cockatoo has become for me the embodiment of a lost opportunity to give meaning to our surroundings beyond the superimposed – and often irrelevant – European view of nature that dictates our relationship with our surroundings. Stands of banksia and mustard yellow Christmas Tree are routinely bulldozed to make way for new suburban gardens full of palms and rose bushes and cats. So the black 'oo-lack' bird resorts to foraging for seed in remnant stands of pine-plantation-turned-housing-estate outside Fremantle; the native geranium and hakea seeds they once favoured are largely gone.

It is hardly a new observation that non-indigenous Australians in general have an uneasy relationship with their own country. For this whitefella, my own sense of dislocation has been with me for a long time. I grew up in Glen Waverley, an upwardly mobile part of outer suburban Melbourne where the landscape seemed to change so regularly that I recall feeling a desire to leave it as soon as I could. Over a decade, orchards next door disappeared, houses were built and then built on to, gardens planted and endlessly re-manicured, and roads widened over years into formidable highways.

I can remember wanting somehow to 'connect' with the place, to make more sense of it, but I couldn't put my finger on how it might happen. There were so few clues to the past, like a row of pines marooned next to a large traffic intersection where a homestead had been until the urban sprawl overtook it. Once there was even some archaeological activity to do with Aboriginal occupancy, which rated a mention in the local paper. The news left little impact; like my immediate environment, it was for me vaguely interesting but ultimately irrelevant, for I would move on.

Later, when I arrived in the Northern Territory in my early twenties, I felt an exhilaration about the landscape I had never before experienced. Slashing wet-season rain carved fast-flowing channels in garden beds and tropical plants grew in riotous profusion. Darwinites had long abandoned irrelevant European terms like 'winter' or 'spring' in favour of two simple concepts, the Wet and the Dry.

But it was 'down the track', out in the bush, where I became aware of another way of 'reading' the country. The Gagadju people living in Kakadu National Park, I discovered, could identify nearly a dozen distinct seasonal changes through 'reading' signs in the bushlife around them. I idly wondered if such 'vision' could be taught, and if so how it could influence non-Aboriginal attitudes to the landscape.

I learned that vast tracts of the physical landscape in the Top End had been transformed over thousands of centuries by Aboriginal people, through careful fire burns (a practice now adopted by modern park managers because scientifically 'proven'). The clues to a once-different landscape were pointed out to me, tiny stands of tropical plants between rock outcrops protected from fire and so hence surviving down the millennia.

Armed with this insight, I stood on a rock surveying with new eyes the 'evidence' of interactive Aboriginal occupation, witnessed by every plant, every tree in the landscape spread out before me. The term 'terra nullius', meaning that the continent was unoccupied when white men arrived, suddenly was nonsense. It was like a magician's trick, as if I could 'see' things in the landscape previously invisible to me. But like so many other white Australians, my contact with that place and those Aboriginal people was short-lived and superficial; the beginning of an understanding soon faded.

I have since had many tantalising glimpses of the 'invisible' in my contact with Aboriginal people over the years. In a small North-West town on a hot summer night, I attended a Baptist church service and sat watching neatly dressed Aboriginal worshippers singing, fussing over their children and praying. I felt as if I had come to another country, as foreign to my own Australian experience as if I were sitting in a prayer meeting in America's deep south.

Afterwards, I sat talking to some children. Cheeky and confident, they pointed out their relatives in the crowd, told me about their school and about where they were born. One boy said he was a 'barramundi'; I didn't understand. The older children tried to explain but I could only grasp hazily that it was something to do with the circumstances of a child's conception and birth. I wanted to know more, wanted to glimpse a little better this child's confident relationship with his 'totem'. But I and my media colleagues had to move on in the restless fashion of all visiting whitefellas. 'Wee-lah, wee-lah', the ghost of this 'other' understanding had gone.

Later working as a journalist on a daily current affairs program in Perth, I dimly became aware that this 'other' version was especially important in Western Australia. Almost every story I was assigned had an Aboriginal dimension, whether about land ownership, welfare, justice, resource development or government administration. I increasingly felt like a person steering a ship through a submerged coral reef. Like most of my professional colleagues, I was a relative newcomer and knew little of what had gone before in my adopted State. It was like reporting in a country whose history, customs and people were only half-visible.

Yet how could I grasp the intensity aroused by mining and land disputes up north without some knowledge of the titanic Noonkanbah clash, and the Aboriginal attachment to land that precipitated it? What could I understand of Aboriginal attitudes to authority – or white attitudes towards Aborigines – without knowing a little of the Moore River Settlement north of Perth, where Aborigines were taken for decades 'for their own good'?

Some information remained 'invisible' for years. It was three years before I discovered that Perth's most popular tourist spot, Rottnest Island, had been a cruel and terminal prison for hundreds of Aboriginal prisoners late last century, a fact still unknown to hundreds of tourists visiting the tiny offshore resort. The dark side of the island's history is now becoming 'visible' to non-Aborigines in a dramatic way, as burial grounds are unearthed only metres from tents and ablution blocks.

I learned in conversation with one interviewee about the long-standing policy of removing half-caste children from their Aboriginal parent, to be brought up among whites. Throughout our conversation, I had assumed the practice had stopped long ago until the man, in only his late thirties, casually mentioned that he had been one of those children.

Like other journalists, I became determined to get 'an Aboriginal point-of-view' on relevant issues, but I couldn't understand why even community leaders were often not readily accessible by telephone. An Aboriginal friend explained it was because she kept receiving calls late into the night from people seeking help with medical, legal or family problems. Although the statistics about poor Aboriginal health and high prison numbers were familiar to me, this episode was the starkest reminder that crisis and instability are a regular feature for many Aboriginal people.

Why does it matter if the vast majority of Western Australians fail to 'see' the existential beliefs, interrelationships and past experiences of a small percentage of its population? The obvious answer is that social justice requires such recognition, but my personal response is an entirely selfish one. Our lives, our places and our past, present and future, can be enriched by knowing our 'other' selves.

But how do you convey such vague ideas to people for whom Aboriginality has, for as many generations as they can recall, been an irrelevance or a nuisance? A case in point can be found in a small rural town, two hours south-east of Perth, where recently the local shire sought to commemorate white civic pride and a hundred years of local government.

The nominated project, a memorial centenary park to be created out of a long strip of derelict land cutting the town in two, was coordinated by a small design team who canvassed townspeople's views, from the Apex Club to the local schoolteacher and the devoted custodians of the local museum. But these people all lived on one side of the town and the design team soon realised that the townsfolk were divided in other ways.

On the other side of the parkland lived a small group of long-term Aboriginal residents. The wasteland in between kept them apart and, although it was nobody's deliberate intention, the Aborigines were the 'invisible' part of the equation. So the design team, whose aim was to include all townspeople's ideas about what to do with the park, spent a memorable afternoon sitting on the front lawn of an elderly Aboriginal resident who recalled the days when the six o'clock curfew required all Aborigines to leave the town precinct.

As a result, a sundial was designed in the park precinct as a reminder to every passer-by that if their shadow pointed to six o'clock, and if they had been Aboriginal, it was once the hour they must be out of town.

Other Aboriginal residents recalled the days when, under cover of darkness, people prepared for corroborees in the wasteland. These memories, this 'other' life of the town, have been commemorated in small 'milestones' made by local Aboriginal design students. Other paving stones marking significant European events in the town's past were made by schoolchildren, and the combined histories were laid throughout the park, a shared heritage made 'visible'.

I do not know if the town is still a town divided. The park project, which is ongoing, has brought groups together, but the design team are not social engineers and decades of mutual distrust are not swept away easily. But one can say that the town's past is now accurately signposted in common ground rebuilt and re-created by its entire population, including the Aboriginal community, so that all aspects of the town's life have been legitimised for the first time.

In general, whitefella attitudes towards indigenous Australians have undergone enormous change and Aboriginal views are increasingly being heard. The Mabo High Court judgment and its implications will continue to dominate and polarise opinions throughout this decade, and I agree with those who describe it as our biggest test of nationhood.

But my personal concern is with a wider community view,

stubbornly persistent, that 'true' Aboriginal people must remain immutably fixed in their past. Urban Aboriginal people are considered 'suspect' by some whites, even media professionals, who refer to them with depressing regularity as 'part-black stirrers' or 'not really Aboriginal'. Only tribal people, apparently, are worthy of respect; if they 'compromise' themselves by using a car or seeking access to social welfare benefits, they are criticised. Why is white Australia incapable of accepting that contemporary Aboriginal culture, like any other, adapts endlessly? It has, after all, been the secret of their survival as a people.

This question is a profound puzzlement to me, as an Australian for whom the celebration of difference, of 'ethnicity', is part of Australia's modern cultural landscape. It is a strong part of my sense of being Australian; like many people my age, I have travelled and lived in Asia and Europe, studied an Asian language and acquired a passing familiarity with European ones.

Multi-culturalism is not merely not threatening to me, it is positively embraced as giving richness to my life as an Australian. I have intimate daily contact with an Italian family, have participated in their family rituals and grown to love the subtle cultural 'hybridisation' of Italian and Australian habits, aspirations, dogmas.

Hybrid culture is accepted by current-day Australians whose parents only yesterday made life miserable for newcomers to Australia. And we do not condemn them to live in the past. That many Italians no longer tend market gardens, or are devout Catholics, or even speak Italian, is accepted. That many now live dramatically different lives in comfortable suburban houses with barbecues in the backyard and a boat is not puzzled over. They are Australian and Italian, and the two are not mutually exclusive. Times change, and so do people. Why, I often ask myself, are Aboriginal people not accorded the same right?

I clearly remember seeing *The Dreamers*, a play by Aboriginal playwright Jack Davis, and its revelatory impact as it depicted an urban Aboriginal family. At that time (more than a year after arriving in Perth) I had not yet met such a family.

Davis' mini-masterpiece showed a close-knit group feuding and making up, tackling the daily obstacles of poverty, ignorance and racism with extraordinary resilience and an astonishing and unique brand of humour. Richly funny slang terms and smatterings of Noongar language punctuated the play, hundreds of words for trees, birds, parts of the State that I knew but never knew by those names. Why had almost none of these words and phrases slipped into whitefella Western Australian parlance?

I sat watching the play in astonishment. Here was an urban Aboriginal culture entirely distinct from the traditional communities of Arnhem Land, yet uniquely Aboriginal just the same. This was an 'ethnic' group with distinct social and cultural mores, yet quintessentially Australian. I have since met many urban Aboriginal families, and as I sit in their loungeroom I am aware of a way of family interaction, a set of values, shared experiences and interests akin to mine but as distinctively different in detail as those of my Italian friends. Why is one form of ethnicity so accepted, another so little understood?

The other day I stood in my child's primary school where the walls were festooned with posters about Aboriginal people and children's paintings attempting to depict a culture more foreign than the Italian or Greek heritage of several classmates. The predominant colours were black, red and yellow, the images puzzled, cliched. I felt only half reassured; the intention was good, the depth of understanding measurable in millimetres. The message seemed to be that Aboriginal people are not alien, but it was not that 'they are us'.

This is our challenge. In Western Australia, in some ways it is easier than in the rest of Australia because the evidence of a linked past is all around us, if we can 'see' it. We have an abundance of prolific writers and talented playwrights who have begun to tell us about our 'other' selves, and the effect on Aboriginal people of our past denial. Family trees are being rewritten everywhere; into my own extended family has come the recent 'revelation', after years of denial, that two generations back, a formal marriage between white and black occurred and children were born. The fact of a common family surname and lives that have intersected give a new perspective to one's interrelationship with a whole group of people once viewed as 'the other'.

It is an experience being repeated all over the State, described in works of literature like Sally Morgan's *My Place* and turned into popular folklore by the highly acclaimed Aboriginal hit musical *Bran Nue Dae*. Sitting in an audience and 'seeing' familiar places and aspects of the past in a new light is an unforgettable experience. I feel increasingly hopeful that my children, and their children, will not experience the sense of dislocation I felt growing up in another part of Australia.

To some extent, non-Aboriginal Australians must live with the legacy of the damage caused by our separateness from Aboriginal people, just like the callous assault on our natural heritage through whitefella indifference. Not everything can be undone; the white-tailed black cockatoos might one day fail to appear in the greying autumn skies, their lives made impossible by unwelcoming suburbs and denuded wheatbelt country. Perhaps we will notice them once they have disappeared, those symbols of our neglected common heritage. Their cry is my cry, 'Wee-lah, wee-lah'... 'Tell me more, tell me more'...

5

THINKING IN AUSTRALIAN

Ted Egan

In the 1940s, during the war, I was a kid selling papers on the trams that came in and out of Coburg, a northern suburb of Melbourne. The city heaved with wartime activity, and service personnel came to and from the war in thousands. Unfortunately wartime can be euphoric, and the powerbrokers trade on this, as they convince people that war will solve problems. It is an exciting time. Songs are written, parties are wild and exuberant, the grog flows free and hopes run high, especially when people are as far removed from the maiming and destruction as we were in Melbourne. I used to chant the many headlines as I swung on and off the trams.

Yet the most memorable day of the war for me occurred when I leapt onto a Number 20 tram with my armful of *Heralds*. 'Heroodapaper' I monotoned, and then stopped in my tracks. All eyes on the tram were on two New Zealand soldiers, both slightly tipsy. They were singing, and they looked great. I had never seen jungle greens before, nor the lemon-squeezer hats the Kiwis wore. One was a Maori, the other a Pakeha, but their complexions looked similar, for both had been taking atabrine tablets to prevent malaria. They were a sallow yellow but, at the same time, stunningly fit.

I have no idea what they were singing, except that it was in the Maori language. Their voices blended in wonderful harmony, and they were obviously just so proud of who they were. I stood, motionless, right in front of them and stayed on the tram. I forgot all about selling papers, and stood, transfixed, until they got off the tram at the Sarah Sands Hotel in Brunswick, and staggered off for more grog. I had to go through the motions of selling papers on the return tram to Coburg, but could not get the singers out of my mind. I had been reared in a family where singing happened easily. I was so impressed.

I wasn't aware at the time but it was the awakening in me that Australia, too, could have a dual heritage, where we whitefellas could be proud of the fact that there was a prior and ongoing Australian heritage to this land, one that really related to the country, unlike the spurious British 'culture' which had been imposed.

It seemed like fate that I was later attracted to Darwin, arriving when I was seventeen. I knew I was still in Australia, yet it was nothing like the Melbourne of my childhood. There were people of all races, and everybody seemed to fit in fairly well. There was a social and legislative system which enabled some whitefellas, the 'silvertails', to feel they were superior to the blackfellas and the Asians; but in important areas like sport, music and commerce the Aboriginals, the Chinese, and the many people of mixed race showed just who were the best.

It was very easy for young Ted Egan to mix freely with all sections of the community without sanctions or inhibitions, and I began to make the contacts that culminated in the many lifelong friendships I cherish so much today. Particularly as I get older and understand real values, I am grateful for the opportunities I had in my impressionable youth. I just wish everybody could have had the same experiences.

I didn't just set out to be a 'blackfella lover'. I mixed freely with all sections of Darwin society, and came to know and respect Chinese, Filipinos, Malays and others, as well as finding compatibility with the many white people who did coexist happily and indeed thrived in the delightful, multiracial fruit salad that Darwin was and still is.

At the same time I was exposed to the considerable Aboriginal presence in Darwin in those days, particularly the

Tiwi people from Bathurst and Melville Islands. They worked for the army and the Royal Australian Air Force, and there was always a large number of Tiwi people around the Catholic Church, which was opposite the ominously named Belsen camp, where I lived. ('Belsen' was an old army camp, on the present site of the Catholic Cathedral.)

Being a Melbourne boy, I bought a football and used to kick 'end to end' with a few mates from Belsen. From nowhere, as soon as we started, we were joined by a few Tiwi blokes, and were they any good? Every day thereafter they would join us, and we all became good mates. I was eventually asked by the Bishop of Darwin to start a footy team and enter it in the Darwin competition, to provide the opportunity for Tiwis from Bathurst Island Mission to play a bit of sport while in Darwin. There was mild opposition to the admission of the team, but eventually, in 1951, the St Mary's Football Club began.

Aged nineteen, I was the first captain, and it was one of the most important things to happen in my entire life. The overwhelming majority of players in our team were Tiwi, and they had stunning whitefella names like Saturninus, Pancratius, Tarcisius and Raphael, for it was the practice on Bathurst Island for them to be baptised with the names of early Christian saints. Later they adopted 'old grandfather' names as surnames, names like Kantilla and Tipiloura, Kerinaua and Apuatimi. Much better stuff.

As well as enjoying the football, and starting a team which forty plus years later absolutely dominates the Darwin competition and has provided great players like Dave Kantilla, Billy Roe, Maurice Rioli and Michael Long to southern clubs, my involvement with St Mary's Football Club introduced me to the man who was to become a profound influence on my life and thinking. His name was Aloysius Puantulura.

At the time we started the footy team Aloysius was employed by the Customs Department in Darwin. Most of the Commonwealth departments had an old Aboriginal man employed, as much a 'presence' as anything else. Aloysius was always immaculate in his starched, long white trousers and white shirt, the 'Darwin rig' of the time. With his jettest of black skin, his beaming smile and great dignity, he played paterfamilias to all and sundry. He would welcome visitors, find out their business, and show them to the appropriate officer with a great flourish. They were great personalities, those 'black eminences' of Darwin, and they did not take any nonsense from anybody in the community, no matter how important people might imagine themselves to be. There was Aloysius at Customs, Johnny Driver at Government House, Tipperary at the Courthouse, Bismark at the Police Station. Wonderful characters, all of them.

Aloysius took me under his wing. 'It's good you start the "play football" for we', he said one afternoon. 'Now I teach you my language, my story, my song.' Thus began my schooling. Most nights I would stroll across from Belsen to the hut where Aloysius, his wonderful wife Mena, and a couple of other old Tiwi lived while in Darwin. He instructed me to bring a book. 'I'm not read and write', he said, 'but I got plenty word, plenty song, plenty story. I want you bookim down.' Away we went. He taught me by singing little rote learning patterns, chanting, Gregorian style:

Ngia, nginta, ngara, nguwa, wuda
(I, you, he/she, we, they)

I think one of the reasons why the Tiwi responded so readily and quickly to the teachings of the Catholic Church was that their own singing is very similar to Gregorian chanting. At ceremonies an individual Tiwi will dance into the ring and deliver a jaw-breaking line like:

Naka wungara ngampurupuwa ngulintinginni ampitimpura waia turuwa

The line is repeated a couple of times, by which time everybody is expected to be word perfect, and join in. Additionally the

Tiwi love the ceremonial aspects of Catholicism – the vestments, the incense, the candles, the ceremonies themselves. And transubstantiation was easy to understand for people who could change themselves into totemic beings. 'Of course I become a yirikapai [crocodile] when I do my dance', said Aloysius. So what's difficult about changing bread and wine into the Body and Blood of Christ?

I quickly became very good at the language, and still delight in being able to visit Nguiu (Bathurst Island) and join in songs and general chatter, to the surprise of young Tiwi kids who ask, 'Who's that old muruntani [whitefella]. How did he learn our language?'

When playing football it was only natural, I felt, to try to talk to the Tiwi players during a game in their own language. Their English was inadequate, and besides, they obviously 'thought' in Tiwi. So especially with terms appropriate to football it became a natural process for me, too, to think and express myself in Tiwi. Many years later and a long way from the Top End I still think in Tiwi in some situations. I have always thought of it as thinking and speaking in 'Australian' rather than in the 'foreign' language English.

Fortunately for me, Paul Hasluck attended the football in Darwin one day. He was Minister for Territories at the time. He heard me giving the half-time peptalk. 'Ingarrdi pakateringa ingani. Pipa, pipala! Yiruka!' (It's a wet day, so mark the ball on your chest. And kick straight down the middle'.) (It's a great language: 'yiruka' means 'straight down the middle of the ground'.) Mr (later Sir Paul) Hasluck came to me after the game, which we had won, and handsomely.

'I'm very interested in both sport and Aboriginal people', he said. 'Would you like to work among Aboriginal people?' I was already a clerk with the Northern Territory Administration, and told him so. He arranged for me to be transferred to what was called in those days the 'Native Affairs Branch'. It was all very long-white-socks and colonial, for they were trying to imitate the New Guinea system of 'native administration' in a country nothing like New Guinea. I was appointed a Cadet Patrol Officer.

There was no system of training, so I was left pretty much to my own devices. I began to operate in a manner which characterised the next twenty-seven years of my public service career. Go and find something interesting to do. Do it, and tell the superiors later. I began to travel around the Top End, to places like the Tiwi Islands, the Cobourg Peninsula, and along the Arnhem Land coast. Most transport was by sea in those days, and it was only a matter of keeping sweet with the skippers of the various luggers and other small craft, and it could all be put down as 'going on patrol'. Thus I would spend weeks on end in the bush living with various Aboriginal communities and on Missions and Government Settlements.

At no stage did I ever feel superior to Aboriginal people, as I noticed a lot of white people did. On the contrary, almost every situation marked me down as the inferior being. Here was this young smart-arse from Melbourne, who thought at first he knew everything, but every day was discovering he knew nothing about the real Australia. As with sport, I was a good learner, and my teachers, especially Aloysius, were at all times patient with me as we began to share our skills.

I was handy to them as I could read and write, and had access to various whitefella agencies. They taught me how to live in the bush, to relax, to have a good laugh, and not to get my bowels in a knot over unimportant things. 'She'll be right' is an outlook we all like to think is 'typically Australian'. Well, believe me, whether we like to acknowledge it or not, we have inherited this laconic approach to life from the first Australians. And so many of our other 'unique' characteristics. I was just one of the mob, no better, no worse than anybody else. 'Tidiganni' is my given name, blackfella-style.

So how is any of this romantic stuff relevant today, when we keep being told that everything in Aboriginal affairs is 'a problem'? Well, let us establish a few starting points. Let's be honest enough to acknowledge that they wouldn't have had too many problems in this country prior to 1788. The sick would have died or got better. The species would have been genetically sound on the basis of a good climate, an adequate and balanced diet, the process of natural selection and the ingenious marriage laws they implemented to enable them to live in small societies without inbreeding. (The crowned heads of so-called civilised Europe could not work that one out, could they? They finished up inbred and prone to genetic diseases like haemophilia.)

Prior to the arrival of the whitefellas, Aboriginal people certainly knew how to live off the land and the sea. It was more a case of 'living with' the elements rather than exploiting them, for they had to develop a religious and ceremonial system which at all times taught them to respect the land, and to control their population and activities accordingly.

They certainly didn't ask the whitefellas to come to Australia. Nor did the arrogant British see fit to ask anybody's permission: they just landed and assumed they had the right to take over.

Blind Freddy could see that our indigenous people have been dispossessed, and shafted absolutely by political interference and the bureaucratic dominance of church and state authorities. The greatest single need is to depoliticise their lives, and allow them the opportunity to start their own recuperative and healing process. This is why we should welcome and celebrate the Mabo decision, for the very wise High Court judges have given Australia its last chance to right the wrongs of the past in a realistic and practical way. But let us determine to keep 'Mabo style' issues out of the courts by confronting all potential litigants with the question 'Could you afford to lose?'

Let the Prime Minister, who does have constitutional power, show the way to a nationally negotiated resolution of these issues. Let us forever recognise that Aboriginals and Torres Strait Islanders are our indigenous people. Let us be proud of that and ask them to apply their traditionally acquired wisdom to the running of a better Australia.

Our indigenous people need more than anything an economic base and this can only be achieved via land, and, in the case of the coastal and Islander people, the sea. Such a base will allow them the opportunity to throw off those aspects of the government handout system which not only keep them mendicant and dispossessed, but also provide grist for the mill of those who delight in vilifying our indigenous people as inferiors, not good enough to be given slices of 'our' Australia on the grounds that they would only stuff it up.

Does not Mr Hugh Morgan (a senior Western Mining Corporation executive and prominent critic of the Mabo decision) point to the failure of Aboriginal people to invent the wheel (did the Welsh?), build houses and towns, and mine minerals as sure indicators that they are backward, second-rate people? How can they compare to the civilisations of Europe? he asks. Europe, which gives us Nazi skinheads, communist thugs and Yugoslavian madmen as manifestations of what 'civilisation' is all about. Give me Aloysius Puantulura as a civilised man any time.

But, our media-frightened Australians say, Aboriginal people are so unreasonable. If we start honouring them as the first Australians, won't they become impossible? Won't they start demanding that the whitefellas, 'rice-crunchers' and others go back to where they came from?

Well, a small minority of whitefella-haters among the Aboriginal people might try that sort of stunt, but they should immediately be asked for some chapter and verse. They simply must not be allowed to get away with the nonsense that all of you whitefellas shot my grandfather and raped my grandmother and stole my sacred sites. The cold, stark, awful truth is that for many Aboriginal people, it is their own ancestors, their own white ancestors that is, who did any shooting and raping that occurred. So let's start looking in a few mirrors before we start apportioning blame.

In my experience, the vast majority of Aboriginal people realise and accept that whitefellas are not going to leave, nor should they. Most are aware that the majority of landholders in Australia have acted honestly in acquiring their possessions, despite the illegality of the original British takeover. In many cases there are real friendships, associations, marriages, and family and sporting ties between Aboriginal people and other

Australians. Let us start at this positive base and work out a better and just Australia. Positive attitudes can be inculcated – and I suggest that the preschools of the nation are the place to start – by teaching kids positive things about Australia, to speak Australian, to sing Australian songs, to relate to Aboriginal people not as inferiors, not as superiors, not as patronisers, but as equals. At the same time let them be the first among equals.

And what do we all call ourselves? It's a bit stupid referring to people other than Aboriginal people as 'non-Aboriginal people'. I certainly don't feel non-Aboriginal. Or 'European'. I suppose 'Aboriginal people and other Australians' is okay. We don't have any nationally accepted terms like Maori and Pakeha, and attempts in some quarters to impose words like 'Koori' on a national level are already bringing stern opposition from the various Yolngu, Anangu, Wongais, Nungas, Noongars and Murris around the country who say, 'Hang on, don't call us Kooris'. Similarly the word to describe non-Aboriginal people is hard to achieve. We get called gubs, gubbas, murantawi and balanda, with gadiya being about the widest-spread term for whitefellas, but again, away from the particular regions where the terms apply, we can't expect national acceptance.

I guess that, until somebody comes up with something nationally palatable, about the best we can do is to use words like Koori in Tasmania, Victoria and New South Wales, Murri in Queensland, Nunga in South Australia, and, on a regional basis in Western Australia and the Northern Territory, the dozens of appropriate terms for blackfella currently in use. Whatever Aboriginal people themselves want is probably the best way to go. Officially we can be referred to as Australians and they as Aboriginal Australians. Despite its colonial overtones, I just love the old New Guinea term whereby old hands were dubbed 'Befores'.

In the meantime I'm very happy and relaxed about being known as a whitefella who respects the fact that the blackfellas were here first in Australia. In fact, I'm as proud of duel heritage as were those two Kiwis on the tram in the 1940s.

Wyatua. Finish.

6

FINDING THE HEART'S HOME

Diana Simmonds

As a child I loved a sunburnt country, I ran wild over sweeping plains. There were rugged mountain ranges and my life was punctuated by droughts and flooding rains. But I wasn't an Aussie kid. Life was also punctuated by visits from the local elephants who had a penchant for my mother's painstakingly tended zinnias. And there was the old she rhino who disrupted trips to the river to fetch water if you got her on a bad day. At other times a leopard would come for the dogs and chickens if normal dinner supplies weren't up to scratch. The other big difference in my sunburnt country was that it was mainly populated by black people and I was brought up by and among them. But one thing is the same: there and here, I am an outsider.

Being an outsider – not being seen to belong – and being an outsider in your own land is, in theory, something many Australians should understand somewhere in their hearts. Thousands, maybe millions, of Australians were political, religious and economic refugees at some point and most definitely within living memory of family members. But there seems to be precious little understanding of this as the issues of Mabo, the republic and immigration exercise a powerful and seemingly unacceptable jolt to levels of tolerance in the community.

As a new Australian, who came here from an ancestral background of mixed and often conflicting nationalities – French, English, Kenyan and Afrikaner – I've had cause to feel the extremes of being an outsider. Funnily enough it's not all bad, though if there were a choice, being an outsider would not be an obvious or easy pick.

For a writer, there's a certain perverse exhilaration in outsiderhood – it's the essential position for observation. But for the ordinary human being who is also a writer there's an awful chill to be experienced in not ever quite belonging. Both conditions have been pushed into sharp relief of late as I – and, most likely, millions of others – try to grapple with what's going on in Australian society and what our place might be within it.

Some curious accusations and assumptions have been bandied about Australia lately. Since Mabo the airwaves have hummed with accusations which are assumed without a moment's pause to be correct. Then the assumptions are turned into accusations, also without pause. On the one hand, Australia's Aboriginal peoples have been accused afresh of being 'stone age' and 'troublemakers'. On the other, the diverse members of Australia's European population are derisively seen as interlopers and hopelessly out of touch with nature, the land and all things spiritual. To a degree all of this is true. But to a similar degree, it is also rather silly.

The irony underlying the 'Mabo debate' (which is usually anything but) is that the late Eddie Mabo, in taking the matter of whether or not his people had native title to their lands to the courts, was doing just what Aboriginal people have been urged to do for years and disparaged for not doing: adopting the ways of white society.

Resorting to the legal system to obtain justice is seen as natural and rightful behaviour by the majority of the population, yet when Aboriginal people do the same it's reinterpreted as a combination of mischief, an absolute affront and a threat to the economic future of the country. If it wasn't so serious it would be funny.

In the early 1960s in the parts of Africa still coloured Empire-pink on school atlases, a similar cosmic joke was in the process of being played on British settlers and their colonial administrations. Black Africans, for long derided as primitive monkeys just down from the trees, were busy graduating from the English education system, with inexorably terminal results for Britain and its colonists.

The parallels with the British tribe of Australia are many and they would do well now to consider that little bit of seemingly remote history. Right now it is primarily this tribe whose men, particularly the elders, still hold the economic and political power, or think they should. They are failing to come to terms with and understand the movement and progress of Australian society. For me they are epitomised by that peculiarly Anglo-Australian institution, the Returned Services League (RSL).

With no exceptions that I've yet come across, RSL clubs, no matter where they're situated – rich streets, poor streets, urban or rural – were specifically designed to ruin any streetscape, anywhere. Their appearance symbolises the attitude of many of their members. They are defiantly, aggressively tasteless; they do not seek to fit in with their neighbourhoods, nor to be a harmonious part of their communities. (And they were also fitted out internally by interior decorators from hell, with much purple vinyl, flock and gilt and high altars of banks of pokies, but that's another story.)

One Saturday morning, not long ago, I went into my local RSL to place a bet on a friend's horse. This club – like so many – is situated on a prime piece of real estate but has the architectural and aesthetic appeal of a 1960s public lavatory. Although there is only a guano-streaked field piece and a faded flag outside, the place has the ambience of the last redoubt. A threadbare wisp of the past, it bristles with hostility and the barbed wire of social rules and regulations. There is something of the world of No unaccompanied ladies, No Jews, No blacks, No thongs, No hats, No long hair; Medals will be worn, Frocks will be worn, Lounge suits only, God save the King and God help the rest. On that otherwise peaceful morning those imperatives hummed in the atmosphere, permeating the very walls, rendering strangers radioactive and sweating.

On this particular Saturday, gathered in one corner of the parquet, was Sandy Stone, his mates and their lady wives. Actually it wasn't Sandy Stone – who was a silly old twit but basically a kindly soul – this man brandished his tinny at the interlopers and bellowed: 'Harroff harroff harroff!' His face was mottled and contorted, he was obviously not greeting us kindly. Eventually it became clear that we should remove our hats.

In my mother's day at least, a lady wouldn't have dreamt of entering a social club without a topping of tulle. To be fair however, in my mother's day a lady wouldn't have been seen dead in public wearing jeans, a sweatshirt and a baseball cap. Bareheaded we passed beneath the smiling eyes of a very young Queen and the choleric glower of her loyal subjects. We managed to resist the impulse to turn and run and marched firmly to the TAB counter. All the while a low grumble revealed that the friendly gent was ruminating on whether we were boys or girls and whether 'that one' was an Abo?

Later that day the horse came home by a nose at fourteen-to-one but it didn't wipe out the unpleasantness of the brush with our village's finest. It also jolted loose other, long-buried memories. It had been the kind of encounter I'd first experienced by inadvertently sitting in the 'Nie Blankes' part of a Transvaal bus during a visit to my South African grandmother in the 1960s. The nonplussed (and probably frightened) black passengers had ignored me while the whites, up the front, rumbled like approaching thunder. The bus went nowhere until finally the driver lumbered down the aisle to put me right – in a 'Blankes' seat where I seethed inwardly at my cowardice, shame and inaction. To wonder how the black passengers felt didn't occur to me at the time. I just knew I wanted to get the hell out of that disgusting society and never return. Ironic, then, that I should later choose to live in the whitest nation on earth.

When, at the age of eighteen, I left Kenya for London – like generations of colonial kids – to see if its streets were paved with gold and to become a writer, my heart broke. I knew I would never be able to go home again, except as a visitor, because of an accident of birth and the colour of my skin. The pain of that knowledge and loss was crushing and my heart hurt for years before finally subsiding to a dull ache that I could live with and mostly ignore. Only when I looked out of a window onto concrete, or rain, or wintry streets, still half-expecting wide bright horizons of bush or ocean, did I despair.

Gradually I began to understand that despite my accent and partial ancestry and enormous efforts to 'fit in', I would never be at home, never belong in England, that small grey wet cold country of some of my genes but not of my soul. It was an uncomfortable bit of intelligence which lurked at the back of my mind for years, unacknowledged. Finally it burst into dazzling realisation, to become more liberating than daunting, the day I landed in Australia for what was supposed to be a holiday.

Years before when arriving at London's Heathrow Airport I'd been shocked by the sea of white faces revealed as the doors separating passengers from greeters slid open. Over the years the shock receded – not least because I'd gravitated unconsciously towards multi-racial areas of the city. So landing in Australia was a double shock: to set foot once again in a predominantly white society – and, at the same time, to 'recognise' the landscape so instantly and so profoundly from my youth. The sense of home was overwhelming as the geography and climate sent tidal waves of relief sluicing through my memory's deepest recesses, uncovering the cognisance of loss of place and longing for home which I had so carefully buried in the hope that they'd go away and stop bothering me.

Now, although still an outsider I am at home in my heart and head – the only way the dispossessed can be. It is a potent sense of belonging. It has a lot to do with red dirt on bare feet and the way wind sounds in dry grass after crossing an entire continent; my belief is that it goes back through generations.

Meanwhile, the residents of the RSL up the road fear to look at the red heart of this country and its wondrously diverse new generations. Instead they peer fretfully out to the sea, towards a motherland that no longer exists and which couldn't care less anyway. At the going down of the sun they will remember very little after a hazy day spent upending tinnies and railing against fate and what has become of the Empire they fought and died for.

Though never really articulated before and probably not even afloat in the collective consciousness, the freedom they marched off to defend was not only freedom from Hitler and Tojo, but freedom from having to contend with uppity Abos, pesky women, flaming foreigners and anyone else who threatened the comfort of their perceived status quo. And this despite a lifetime of humanitarian heroism from such latterday saints as Weary Dunlop and hundreds of unknown others.

Unfortunately for those who would wish the status quo was set in concrete, history shows that it is one of the things about humankind that remains forever fluid. Empires come and empires go, armies are disbanded by old age and changing circumstance. The meek may well inherit somewhere along the line and that means that the uppity Abos, the pesky women and the flaming foreigners are here and are the future.

And the outsider ... well, the outsider probably always remains outside, but warmed by an inner glow at the tenacious quality of humour and the indomitability of the human spirit.

7

A LATE LEARNING

Hal Jackson

Growing up in the 1940s and 1950s, I was not conscious of being anything other than 'Australian'. I now suppose that in or near the small country towns of Victoria where I lived there were Aboriginal families, but I wasn't aware of them. Later, as a teenager in Melbourne, I met my first 'coloured person' – Jesse Owens, the famous runner covering the Melbourne Olympics for his newspaper. By then I had, of course, heard of people like Lionel Rose and Doug Nicholls*, two famous Aboriginal sportsmen.

But such individuals were rare – Aboriginal people were out of my sight and out of my mind, as I'm sure they were among the bulk of my contemporaries. I recently returned to my old school and talked to some of the students. I suspect things have not greatly changed.

The issues in the Australia of my youth were those of Protestant and Catholic, labour and capital. As the son of a suburban family with a bank manager father, I was brought up in the tradition of a Protestant God, an English King and white middle-class values. To the extent that Aboriginal people were ever mentioned, at home, in school, or in our general community, it was as a dying barbaric people.

Our duty as a society was to hand out relief and, to use a com-

---

* A boxer, Lionel Rose won the World Bantamweight title in 1969. Douglas Nicholls, later Governor of South Australia, was a professional runner and an Australian Rules footballer.

mon phrase of the time, 'smooth the dying pillow'. To the extent that we thought about it at all, we would have had no problem in agreeing with Manning Clark's introduction to the first of his six-volume history of Australia. He asserted that civilisation came to Australia in the last quarter of the eighteenth century. And in so agreeing, we would not have felt it necessary to define civilisation as necessarily centring on the growth of cities, and the sorts of structures and economy which make them possible.

Later, as a teenage university student, I moved with my family to Perth. Again I had little exposure to cultural diversity. In my years at Law School there were two Singaporean women and a Zambian. I do not recall any Aboriginal students. Nor to my knowledge were there any courses, other than in the Anthropology Department then newly established by Professor Berndt, which mentioned Aboriginal history, culture, language or place in Australian society. Certainly I do not remember any such mention in the unit on Australian history which I took towards a Bachelor of Arts degree.

I knew nothing of the matters Archie Roach sings of:

> This story's right, this story's true
> I would not tell lies to you
> Like the promises they did not keep
> And how they fenced us in like sheep
> Said to us Come take our hand
> Sent us off to mission land
> Taught us to read, to write and pray
> Then they took the children away.

In legal terms my consciousness of Aboriginal issues developed only slowly. In 1971 the decision in *Milirrpum v. Nabalco Pty Ltd*, which ruled against Aboriginal customary title to land surviving British annexation of the continent, was no legal surprise. Nor was it a matter of great community interest. It affirmed what we had always known. Our cultural isolation meant we knew nothing of contrary trends elsewhere.

What I do recall are the jokes about Allawah Grove and Peppermint Grove – the social extremes of Perth society.

This was also, it should be recalled, the dying era of European colonial dominance. The coloured people of much of the world were still enduring the throes of obtaining political independence and, in many places, the resulting chaos. White assumptions of racial and cultural superiority ran deep. Some people now prominent in Western Australian politics then made no secret of their support for white South African rule and the European colonial empires.

Even living in Perth – a city with proportionately more Aboriginal people than other capitals – I was oblivious to any real Aboriginal presence until at least the 1970s. No doubt social isolation and the control mechanisms then unknown to me were partly the cause. I do recall watching Aboriginal footballers like 'Polly' Farmer, but for me there was no personal contact.

Some of my friends from those days had grown up in rural Western Australia – sons of the wheatbelt. They claimed to understand Aboriginal people, but I have never seen them talking to any Aboriginal person, and their racism is now to me palpable and obvious. Not that they are alone – racism and xenophobia have been endemic at all levels of Australian society.

When non-Aboriginal Australians like myself eventually thought about Aboriginal people and their place in Australia at all, the initial assumption was that Aboriginal people, 'real Aborigines', were 'full bloods' and lived in the desert like Albert Namatjira. In the 1960s and 1970s Western Australian pastoralist and mining millionaire Lang Hancock was to say, unashamedly on television, that the problem was 'mixed-blood' Aborigines and the solution to herd them together, poison their water and sterilise them into oblivion. More recently one woman has claimed to be his mixed-blood daughter. At the time his comments met only modest protest.

Over time I was to learn a little of the diversity of Aboriginal people in modern Australia. I was to learn the resentment of Aboriginal people both at the assumption that Aboriginality requires 'full-blood' ancestry, and at the consequences which sometimes follow for part-Aboriginal people.

In the 1980s, when I was working as a law reformer in Perth, the Australian Law Reform Commission in Sydney was given a reference on Recognition of Aboriginal Customary Law. Such a reference throws that diversity into sharp relief.

A period of service as a judge of the District Court included exposure to the many significant and difficult problems besetting Aboriginal people and their interaction with the legal system – policing, judiciary, juries, sentencing, fines, gaol. Some of these problems can be acute, as events involving an (unsuccessful) application for bail in Kalgoorlie so the defendant could receive a traditional spearing before being sentenced in the Supreme Court attest.

The issues are sometimes before me when sitting in the Children's Court of Western Australia, dealing with Aboriginal children and adolescents from remote areas. Traditional punishments, traditional child rearing and discipline practices, the very concepts of manhood and adolescence, all these can and do conflict with international instruments and modern liberal views for child protection and juvenile justice.

However, none of these things challenged in my mind or those of my colleagues the very basis of European occupation.

What first challenged me in terms of the fundamental issues of the occupation of Australia by non-Aboriginal people was, ironically, my first visit to New Zealand. In 1984 I was to attend meetings of the Law Council of Australia and the Law Societies of Australia and New Zealand in Rotorua – one of the main centres of Maori culture.

The conference started with the Governor-General, a former judge of eminence, approaching a group of local Maori elders assembled on stage and asking them, in what seemed to be fluent Maori, permission to hold the conference in their area. Suddenly I was face to face with a gulf of behavioural expectations between that reality and the Australian experience. How could one imagine any eminent Australian speaking an Aboriginal language? Who would ask Aboriginal elders' permission to hold a function? Later I was to see more of New Zealand, to see Maori language classes on national television, to visit Waitangi and feel the respect for a treaty inconceivable to most Australians. Later again, I was to understand that Aboriginal people pay respect to each other's country in much the same way as I'd seen in New Zealand.

These issues are difficult to conceptualise in the context of most Australians' lives. The issues became much more real for me after I became the first President of the Children's Court of Western Australia. The State Government of the day, with the support of myself and others, established an Advisory Committee on Young Offenders. My duties took me to small remote communities in the outback and northern parts of the State which I'd not previously visited. Some of these visits were to sit in courts. Others were as a member of the committee, now sadly abolished.

In such places the reality of the closeness in time of European occupation becomes much more real. The loss of land and language is tangible. To read history in a book is one thing. To meet people who remember, or whose families remember, is quite another. The people I met helped fill in the reality.

Pat Dodson (a royal commissioner in the inquiry into Aboriginal deaths in custody) told me how a member of his family had seen the first nuns come ashore on the Broome Peninsula, and thought they were giant seabirds because of their habits and headwear. At Kalumburu I spoke to an elderly lady who was the first baby born at the mission. Her mother tongue, spoken only by a handful, is dying out as people like her pass on. I recall one man my own age at Balgo telling how members of his group were made to walk in neck chains from Balgo to Halls Creek.

Non-Aboriginal people have little knowledge of such things. My own knowledge is slight. We all have a good deal to learn because this is our own past too.

But the assumptions made by most white Australians are the most disconcerting result of that lack of knowledge. I was brought face to face with this one night in Broome. At the Cable Beach Club Resort I was introduced by a mutual friend to a tourist visiting from Melbourne. 'How,' he asked, 'do the

Aboriginal people fit in up here?'*

The Mabo decision makes all us whitefellas re-evaluate the basis of questions like that.

The reality of the longer term consequences of occupation also faced me in another form when I took up the position at the Children's Court. Soon after my appointment I visited the juvenile detention centres around Perth. These overcrowded relics of the 1950s housed a mass of young and overwhelmingly black faces. The statistics were reinforced in a graphic and personal way, made more significant and personal because of my new position. I had been to many of the State's adult prisons where the story had been no different. Now I was not just one of a large number of sentencers, but the symbolic head of the judicial system responsible for their incarceration.

I was not then to know the furores that were to follow various attempts to refocus the system. The depth of Aboriginal feelings of injustice was to come to me clearly when I attended a seminar held by the Australian Institute of Criminology soon after my appointment. My attempt to explain the position of the judiciary was perhaps clumsy. I'd hardly started when a group of Aboriginal activists stormed out.

Later I met conflict from other sources. In the report of the Royal Commission into Aboriginal Deaths in Custody (*Regional Report into Underlying Issues*, vol. 1, p. 162), the following passage appears:

It was further stated that the 'Chairman' of the Children's Court:

'in the view of this Union favors Aboriginal kids and in fact the prejudice is now firmly placed in the minds in the rest of the community against the Aboriginal people who are receiving favorable justice or lack of justice ... [RCIADIC Transcript, Police Union, 1990:785]'

---

* About 24,000 people, including 12,000 Aborigines, live in the Kimberley, a region almost twice the size of Victoria.

The Royal Commission report comments:

> It is unfortunate that the Police Union representatives were not more helpful in addressing the real problems faced by this Court, and the juveniles who come before it ...

Backed by these police comments, some sections of the media and some politicians in Western Australia, fanned by tragic events the roots of which they entirely misunderstood (a series of deaths following high speed police chases of stolen cars driven by juveniles), later spent much time and money to organise a rally at which I was to be denounced as 'Public Enemy No. 1' in scenes shown on national television.

During that period I was sustained not only by the support of people I knew both privately and in a range of areas of public life, but by the traditions of the law, now centuries old. This requires judges not only to remain impartial and open-minded in their work of determining individual cases, but to resist the often blatant pressures of the populist parts of the media to seek momentary popularity, and the insidious pressures of government agendas. The general public cannot be expected to understand, without explanation, the needs of courts and judges if the fundamental conditions of a free society are to be supported. Without such sustenance minorities and unpopular individuals are at great risk. However, even with an independent, impartial and open-minded judiciary, the traditional Anglo-centric legal system does not necessarily guarantee an adequate response to cultural difference.

I have already referred to some of the legal issues involving Aboriginal people from remote and more traditional areas, and to common Aboriginal feelings of disenchantment with the justice system. New models need to be found if we are to deal with these issues.

In urban and closely settled Australia, virtually all traces of Aboriginal language and most traditional Aboriginal ways have been lost. There can be no going back. We cannot, even in the most remote parts of the continent, preserve a hunter-gatherer culture like a museum exhibit frozen in time. It is almost all gone, although aspects remain strong and must be respected.

In urban and regional Australia, Aboriginal people must take their place in the twenty-first century. There is no future in the rhetoric of those Aboriginal people who, under the banner of an Aboriginal Provisional Government, urge some form of separate nationhood, or of those who posture loudly as leaders but provide no positive directions and who sometimes denigrate their achieving fellows as 'coconuts' or 'jackies'.

Sometimes the media treat as spokespersons for Aboriginal people those who seem to me to lack credibility. There are many other Aboriginal people achieving quietly in modern Australia those things which will give their people greater recognition and hope. Equality and respect must be willingly given by white Australians, but it will be most readily given to those Aboriginal people who make achievements as citizens of the contemporary world.

This is not to urge a return to policies of assimilation or genocide. It is possible, indeed perhaps essential, not just for themselves but for all Australians, that Aboriginal people both take their place in the future and retain their Aboriginal identity. Anything less would be to diminish all Australians.

White Australians concede cultural diversity to most groups in our nation in terms which are generous by world standards. We must now do so with those who have occupied the continent for tens of thousands of years.

But we must also allow that diversity of history and place which I have mentioned to be reflected in different forms, according to models determined by Aboriginal people. This isn't apartheid. It is to respect cultural diversity and the special claims of Aboriginal people as the original occupants of the land we now share. To recognise this on appropriate terms involves acknowledging the continuance of both land use and cultural heritage in ways promoting mutual respect. Only then will whitefella Australians have the right to say they refuse to acknowledge any debts for the past.

This is not an issue for privatisation or States' rights. It is a national challenge not just for non-Aboriginal people but for Aboriginal Australians.

8

NO QUESTIONS PLEASE, WE'RE AUSTRALIANS

Duncan Graham

The year was 1960, the place Gnowangerup, dubbed Australia's 'Little Rock' by a media scratching for similarities with the Arkansas capital where racism and the enforced integration of schools had provoked riots.

There were no street battles in the place of the gnows, the curious mallee fowl which incubates its eggs in giant mounds. Just a complete rejection of the tags imposed by ignorant outsiders, a sullen acceptance of the way things were by the landless, and a cheerful indifference to the misery and inequalities among the landed who believed this was the way things had been created, a situation ordained by God. Therefore they lived proper lives in a just land.

None of this was immediately obvious to a wide-eyed young man from England who had just found a job pulling a plough behind a bulldozer to 'open new country'. The CP (conditional purchase) land had been bought for two shillings and sixpence an acre as an investment by a city businessman. He'd reluctantly employed a bearded 'new chum' only after heavy moral persuasion by a Commonwealth Bank officer who urged the sour old man 'to be a good Christian'. The employer reasoned, in the simplistic style which tends to be found among rural conservatives, that anyone who didn't shave had to be idle.

(A month later I was sacked, then served a writ alleging my wife Ann and I had taken a pillow from my employer. Though we protested innocence the police advised payment rather than go to court. In those days there was no legal aid. The unfairness rankled for months, but perhaps it predisposed us to a better comprehension of injustice. Again and again I was to find the harsh words and actions of Manning Clark's 'walnut-hearted' Tories creating crusaders for change in their wake. Had the reactionaries taken a milder, more balanced approach to different values, many waverers would have been easily discouraged from further pursuit of the perpetual puzzles, and those showing only amateur concern would never have become professionally involved.)

Every year at that time one million acres of bush was being destroyed, much of it mallee, to make way for wheatlands, an act of development celebrated in the grossest fashion by the State Government. Few seemed aware that the native trees were keeping the salt under control. If they knew, they were unconcerned. Somehow it would all be fixed, it would be okay. If not, there was always plenty of land somewhere else. Anyone inclined to speak out risked being shunned as a crazy. Conservation was a term for museums, not agriculture. Within thirty-three years the situation would reverse with the Western Australian Government urging the planting of mallee to create a eucalyptus oil industry.

But back to the 1960s and the ball and chain pulled by two bulldozers crushing all in its path. Soon freshwater creeks turned saline. Plants became rare or extinct. Wildlife, left without food and shelter, vanished. Species which had been prolific disappeared. Chancing on a gnow, once commonplace, was soon a noteworthy event. Land which given proper husbandry should have grown food to benefit all vomited the poison which it had so long suppressed. It was a metaphor, though at the time unrecognised.

Also invisible, though not literally, were the original Australians of the South-West, the Noongars. At the time they were the natives, and they were there to be ignored, persecuted or exploited, talked about but seldom talked with. It didn't make sense to a newcomer so the town's policeman, with nothing to do one spring afternoon, found time to explain the facts of life in a Western Australian wheat and sheep town, then deliver a homily on local values. This concluded with the warning: 'Don't let me catch you taking plonk to the coons, or going on the Reserve.'

The curious language of this judicial pronouncement needed further explanation. So the raggedly-dressed, dark-skinned people who walked with downcast eyes were not allowed to drink. Why not? It was the law, he said with absolute finality. Natives with liquor were dangerous and untrustworthy. Then he told a lurid tale of a man from the town being disembowelled by a broken bottle in a drunken brawl and being taken to the hospital on the roof of a saloon car.

Presumably he got treatment. If so he was luckier than one brown baby who had to wait in his mother's arms on the doctor's verandah till all the white patients had been seen, even those who arrived after hours. By then it was too late. The doctor was suspended for three months but returned to work with only minor modifications to his practice.

Keeping the natives waiting, out of the swimming pool, in the front row of the movies, segregated at school, shunned in the street, away from the pub and unserved in the tea rooms, even if, like Noel Yarran, they'd just returned from fighting communists in the jungles of the Malay Peninsula, was the style of the town. The doctor's despicable attitude was no different to anyone else's. It was the way things were. It had been written. The conquerors and the conquered. Might was right, and might was white.

Yet these Australians were good church-going folk who celebrated the coming of the Christ-child as redeemer for all, generous and friendly to a newcomer with a funny accent and strange ideas, prepared to give a lift or a loan. Their handshakes were firm and they looked a man in the eye. When a local cocky fell sick, or was injured at seeding or harvest, all would come together to put in, or take off, the crop. At every function the ladies provided a plate, a warming ritual of sharing, a communion recognising we are one and together. But the hands which so generously prepared the riches of this lovely land and the hands which took the bounty were all white.

Everywhere generosity, decency, care and concern. No, not quite everywhere. Why didn't these people, my tribe, rightly famed for straight talk, mateship and the grand gesture, behave in the same way towards those who had been here much longer and were so clearly suffering? In any search for the archetypal Aussie battler it would have been impossible to go past the indigenous people of Gnowangerup. Yet these people were vilified, not celebrated. Why? By then too many knockbacks to my questions had left a bruised ego. Had I asked I doubt any would have understood.

Early one wet morning, the crop sown, the super spread and the sheep crutched, the new boss drove his Land Rover out of town, off the blacktop and through a gap in a barbed-wire fence. This was the Reserve. We bumped down a rutted track not taken before, more creek than road. The vehicle stopped. The horn blared. The boss sat still. Then, in the damp gloom, came movement. I see it now with chilling clarity. Figures from some medieval tableau began to move like monks, cowled in grey superphosphate sacks. They came from low shelters, a weaving of wattle, rusting iron and more stained sacks. These figures, these humans, dripped with wet and shivered with cold. They cringed.

When they spoke to the boss through the driver's window it was in a deferential tone in a language difficult to decipher, a sort of childish, abbreviated English with a strangely rich timbre. The boss told three or four to get inside. I went to move across the seat and open the door. 'In the back'. he muttered with authority, and leant across to keep the door shut. The boss was a man of few words, no sense of humour and no desire to explain or debate. How could people live so close yet be so distant? I had quit my homeland disgusted with a society driven by class and privilege, only to find in Australia a duplicate of the culture I thought could survive only in the 'old' world.

The antipodean version was shaded by the wide-brimmed, corkfringed myth of egalitarianism. You could call the boss by his first name, sit in the front seat and drink at the same bar –

provided you were the same colour. Nothing was making sense.

That day we garnered the gnarled, ancient and twisted mallee roots on 'new' country, and piled them for burning. At smoke-o the boss and I sat on a log and chewed mutton and tomato-sauce sandwiches prepared by our wives. The Noongars (though that term was not in currency) lit a fire and sat elsewhere in a small circle. They appeared to have no food. I wandered across and tried to make conversation. They responded with suspicion and monosyllables.

Every waking moment the questions mounted, building a barrier to communication and comprehension. Every day the logic, the reasoning, the history stayed as far as the Stirling Range, a shadow line of unreachable and distant hills. That was until we met Mona Treasure. She had a small farm largely run by her husband Tup, a portly fellow with a lust for Australian Rules football and beer, a cheerful man though ill-equipped to respond to the questioning Poms. Mona was not so handicapped, for country women seemed less bound by the bushman's taciturn code. Many Noongars were her friends and two were destined to become her daughters-in-law. Some visited her house and worked her property. And they even had another name. They were, she said, though not offensively, 'half-castes', the dispossessed, displaced remnants of the people who had lived here before those who had come with guns and fencing wire and stock. Some of those later arrivals, she inferred, had been characters of low morality, hence the less than pure-black people on the Reserve. Much later I was to discover these inseminators had also been men of high status, pioneers, explorers, politicians, statesmen whose other exploits were taught at school.

(Many years on, when reporting for the *West Australian* newspaper I met Tom Forrest, then the caretaker at the Mount Magnet Reserve in the Murchison. He was, he revealed, the grandson of the famous explorer and one-time mayor of Perth, Alexander Forrest, whose statue, at the junction of Barrack Street and St George's Terrace, gazes north seeking other lands – and women – to conquer. The newspaper refused to publish the interview lest it upset the white section of the family.)

Back in Gnowangerup we were introduced to more Western Australians, though not of Mona's liberal mind, and as upright members of the community surely not the type to father the children who had to be kept out of school for reasons of 'hygiene'. At the local hall where the 'Progress Association' met, a notice above the stove warned against the burning of blackboys. Progressing from what to where? Why did the grass trees have such names? What did it all mean? Why couldn't anyone tell me? (Even the unladen inquiries annoyed. One day I asked the boss why the long-tailed screech of green and yellow which gorged the wheat trucks' roadside spill were called twenty-eights.* The question annoyed. 'Because they are,' he grunted.

Australia was the land of no explanations, or the inexplicable. There was, of course, another possible reason, though it took years to make the discovery. An outsider's delving into the past, questioning the order of things, threatened to blow away the topsoil of comfort and reveal the poisons below.

Then came the heat and the harvest. Several times a day I loaded a truck with bags of wheat, lifted in one stomachcramping jerk from the ground where they'd been dumped off the header. Each sack had to be carefully shaken and nudged tightly into place for the long gravel-corrugated journey to the bin in town. One scorching, brilliant afternoon, bored with the shuffling to-and-fro repetition of the haulage, I stopped the truck and wandered into the mysterious, darkening shade of mottle-barked jam, thin-leafed casuarina and bushy wattle. The hot smooth sand was largely unmarked, except where low hanging branches had whisked the ground clean.

Charmed by the scene, seduced by the warmth and sweat of the eucalyptus, it occurred to me that I might be the first human ever to have trodden this spot. Excited by this prospect I pulled off my boots and put the print of soft, white Anglo-Saxon feet

---

* The Port Lincoln Parrot has a three-syllable call with the last note pitched higher and sounding (to some ears) like 'twenty-eight'.

firmly into the red soil of this strange and exotic land with no answers. The imprint stayed for the soil was slightly damp, and the crust not about to crumble. I thought I had arrived and my skin prickled with the emotion of the moment.

It was, as I now know, an arrogant and absurd gesture founded on ignorance and the brashness of youth. Though unaware of it at the time, stamping my mark duplicated the actions of the 'pioneers' who had 'opened up' the country and 'made the desert bloom', reinforcing the Eurocentric view that Australia was an empty land, a virgin country waiting for its wealth to be stripped and revealed, then taken by the victors who had defeated the unknown and therefore had the right to be there and make the rules.

Slowly the information amassed. It was never readily accessible. Every item had to be gouged, like gold, out of the hard Australian psyche. I went to university and studied anthropology under Professor Ronald Berndt. His barking lecture style, and attempts by his colleagues to fit kinship ties into mathematical models dismayed. Only later was I to learn that on a personal level 'Prof' Berndt and his extraordinary wife Catherine were people enchanted and enriched by the great wisdoms they had discovered through a lifetime's work with Aboriginal people.

(Shortly before his death in 1990, and suffering from cancer, the 'Prof' showed me crayon drawings on brown paper he'd collected during the Second World War, when he had asked old people to record their first-contact memories. His enthusiasm was that of a teenager who had suddenly found love and a world washed fresh with perfect promise. If only other Australians could have shared his understandings, his humility, his unpolluted joy.)

Then into journalism. First job was the Police Courts. On Mondays most defendants were black. The magistrate made no pretence of justice. Instead he shamelessly played to the press bench, fining and gaoling weekend drunks in a silly ritual which made no sense. No legal aid in those days. I questioned my superiors. They said that was the way things were. 'Don't go north of the line at night or you'll get a knife in your ribs,' cautioned colleagues, echoing the warnings of the Gnowangerup policeman. The location of fear was North Perth, then largely inhabited by Italians, Slavs and Aborigines, though such terms were not used. (The language was Eyties, Dagos and Boongs.) North of the railway line which bisected the capital of smug indifference were the cheap wine bars, hovels, humpies of corrugated iron and sacks, a city version of the shame of Gnowangerup.

In the dirty parks lived the crumpled men and women who sought comfort from methylated spirits, 'white lady', and port, sold at inflated prices by the whites who hung around the area, the 'bungee men' who demanded sex for grog. Prohibition was still in force. An olive-skinned 'reffo' could walk off a boat from Europe and into a bar with no questions asked, even if he couldn't speak the language. An Aborigine, born in the land of his ancestors and speaking English, playing sport for the State and fighting for the nation, had no such right. Unless, of course, he held a citizenship certificate, a 'dog licence'.

I was never stabbed north of the line and seldom threatened, except by aggressive drunks too pitiful to be a danger to anyone but themselves, or police suspicious of a young white man in a district many considered a no-go area.

Instead I met people like Jack Davis trying to get the Aboriginal Advancement Council under way, later to become an internationally acclaimed poet and playwright; Elizabeth Hansen running a soup kitchen for her people and being harassed by local government authorities for cooking in a shop which didn't meet petty rules on hygiene. The fact that the living conditions in the parks outside were an affront to every basic health requirement seemed to mean nothing.

There was a wealth of other special people working in the area. Korean War veteran Ken Colbung who had learned the skills of articulate and assertive expression which fazed the government workers in the Native Welfare Department (NWD). This portfolio was shared with Police, a marriage which said much about government attitudes. In the NWD was Norm Harris, one of the first Aboriginal public servants, whose father (also Norm) had mustered a delegation which had confronted Premier Collier in 1928 politely requesting to be treated as equals. There was George Abdullah whose intractable demands for improvements in conditions and services frustrated NWD staff.

Then I met May O'Brien, one of the most outstanding people in the State, who had brilliantly coped with the hassles and qualities of both cultures. The State's first woman Aboriginal teacher who got to the top of her job then let her great talents loose on a wealth of other national and international issues. (Years later at the Western Australian Police Academy, after May had lectured recruits, we shared afternoon tea with a senior sergeant. He thought the time right for a broadbased attack on perceived Aboriginal evils which inevitably included drinking too much and working too little. Astonished at the generalisations I reminded him that May was Aboriginal. 'Oh, sure,' he said without a pause, 'but you're different.' 'No, I'm Aboriginal too,' said May. 'You know what I mean,' said the sergeant as though we shared a common world view.)

Censorship was not confined to the media. The government was also actively involved in keeping the truth suppressed. Dorothy Parker, an academic at The University of Western Australia, persuaded the police to take her on patrols around North Perth and East Perth. In the company of an apparently harmless mature woman (whose son was to become the State's deputy premier of a Labor Government which did little to ease the plight of the people revealed by his mother's research), the police displayed their arrogance and born-to-rule superiority. Ms Parker's embarrassing report was suppressed by the Western Australian Government, then Liberal-Country Party. It took another twenty-five years before such issues and attitudes were to be recognised and officially condemned.

When a small group of Nyangumarta came out of the Western Desert in the mid-1960s and encountered Europeans for the first time at La Grange in the West Kimberley, the chief of staff at the *West Australian* newspaper thought the event too insignificant to send a journalist. Fortunately I have met these and many other people whose lives have been forever changed by the sudden discovery that another race of people has invaded their country and imposed language, culture, technologies and a cosmology beyond imagination.

Some died from the impact. Others adapted and triumphed, learning in years what has taken others millennia to understand. This is stuff of absolute fantasy. It is so enormous, so challenging that no one effort of intellect can hope to circumscribe the implications. Where else in the world can such colossal events occur yet excite such little interest?

In the Western Desert we met people with no English living in wiltjas and who had only recently met the invaders, squatting on stations and missions administered by people who were in some cases humble. More frequently they were arrogant, self-appointed 'experts' who seemed at ease in telling a young journalist how the 'native problem' could be fixed. Their solutions included segregation, crushing the culture, destroying artefacts, keeping people ignorant and dependent, treating the country's indigenous population like animals in a zoo. The 'case of whisky and a box of bullets' solution was frequently encountered, sometimes as a joke, sometimes not. Many carried their Christianity openly but failed to uphold the Christian ethics of tolerance, forgiveness, understanding, compassion and love.

Then, as now, it was tough for anyone offering alternative views. Many, like Don McLeod, who had a different view of the world, were branded communist and 'white stirrers'. He accurately forecast that the story written following an interview at the Twelve Mile Camp outside Port Hedland would never be published by the *West Australian*. As a forceful critic of the local media, and an able litigant in defamation cases, he'd lost the right to be reported in his own State. Fortunately the *Bulletin* was prepared to forgive.

In the Eastern Goldfields we met Sadie Corner, then married to the descendant of Alfred Canning, the man who had 'opened' the desert stock route which bears his name. Ms Corner was a nurse, and a Wongi. Through her we learned about the United Aborigines Mission Mount Margaret Mission and the great achievements of the children who had been educated by Rod and Mysie Schenk and Mary Bennett. People like May O'Brien, Les Tucker, Kathy Trimmer, Aubrey Lynch, Fred Meredith and others who had triumphed against official racism and indifference to become public figures and community leaders.

Were these poets and soldiers, teachers and nurses, administrators and musicians the same people as those who lived in metal shacks on reserves, constantly harassed by the police, treated as imbeciles? How could some people rise above the hostility, shake off the handicaps yet still retain their culture? It's a question which still scratches my mind.

One answer is that these particular missionaries, unlike many of their colleagues and indeed much of the State, believed absolutely that there were no limits to the achievements of the Wongi kids. Yet there was another stage preceding that belief. They recognised that Aboriginal people were human beings with all the qualities and concerns of any other person in the world.* That was something few others were prepared to accept, then and now, where politicians put State rights ahead of human rights.

In the Pilbara and Kimberley we found the same laager-like attitudes which had prevailed in Gnowangerup, though by now the official policy was to close reserves, or at least use them as staging posts on the way to a life inside town limits. This new policy was a gem of a political construction designed more to appease whites than help blacks. It had all the Dr Strangelove qualities of a bureaucracy turned feral. It 'worked' this way: if you could keep an insulated tin shed with a concrete floor clean, tolerate summer heat and winter cold, share a community tap and toilet, ensure the kids stayed nit-free and went to school wearing

---

* Before moving to Mount Margaret, Mary Montgomery Bennett had a book published in London in 1930 entitled: *The Australian Aboriginal as a Human Being*. Mrs Bennett, a widow, was, according to Margaret Morgan, one of the Schenks' daughters, 'considered a radical in her day because of her insistence on human rights for Aborigines.'

smart clothes, if you could pass these tests, accept your lot and not let your bitterness break loose and give the police or the principal or the welfare the sharp side of your tongue, then you might be allocated an old State house on the edge of town where you'd be forever watched for a relapse. Provided, of course, that the local shire agreed and the neighbours raised no objections.

Who dreamed up these policies? On what knowledge and research were they based? No one articulated the reasoning and no one suggested they might have been based on racist notions. It was just the way things were.

In the North-West the stations were busy evicting people from the pastoral leases where they had lived for thousands of years and to no protest from the Crown which owned the country. The reason was the equal wage decision. Till then Aboriginal labour had been rewarded with rations. Now the courts in the south had ruled Aboriginal people were entitled to the same rights as other Australians, in other words to be recognised as human beings. In retaliation graziers ordered the people away, forcing them into the town reserves where there was no work, little shelter and all the ingredients for conflict and social chaos.

The conventional wisdom of the north was that only the 'pioneers' knew what was right, and the 'white stirrers' in the south were destroying everything with their fancy policies, imported from nations jealous of the lucky country. The Aborigines, we were told, were like children. Give them a feed and a plug of baccy, leave them alone and these 'stone age-people' would be happy forever.

The myth was sustained by the media which gave the graziers an unwarranted cachet as custodians of bush values, wise in the ways of nature and humanity who stood at the frontier fighting drought and flood, fire and depression. Then, and now, it remains a fabrication, gainsaid by few.

Back at university most anthropologists seemed content to stay silent. The politicians pontificated. The conventional counter view was that education would soon smother ignorance and all would be enlightened in an evolutionary (but not revolutionary) new age. The trouble with this reasoning was that like evolution, the pace of change away from the city was glacial and that the real agenda was to maintain the status quo.

In Perth things were moving, though manipulating 'outsiders' were blamed. The other tactic was to divide and destroy. The uppity urban blacks were not 'real' Aborigines, who were supposed to stand on desert rocks at twilight, one foot cocked against the other, and not speak out for their civil rights. At Allawah Grove (where taxi drivers often assumed visitors were seeking 'black velvet') the anger was tangible, compounded by bitter factional squabbling which was to last for decades. This reserve on the outskirts of Perth (at Guildford, an ancient camping ground) was soon to be obliterated by the expanding airport. Progress and development, sweeping into the Western world's most isolated capital with a scream of Rolls Royce jets drowning the concerns of those living in squalor.

The same questions raised in Gnowangerup were applicable here in the more sophisticated city. The gulf between the races was just as broad. The government urged, deplored, procrastinated, called for reports, initiated inquiries, made forthright comments with carefully hidden qualifications, appointed new staff, changed department titles, designed fine logos for new letterheads, developed fresh programs but in the end did nothing real and meaningful. To do so would have required an overthrow of long-held beliefs, a revolution of thinking which none were prepared to risk.

The questions asked in Gnowangerup remained unanswered, though there are responses clear as the light that shafted through the eucalypt on that day when I thought my foot was the first to impress one tiny section of Australia.

I know it now, and I now know I knew it then. The answer is land and an unconditional recognition of prior ownership and use, and an unqualified wonder at the way Aboriginal people have prospered and adapted and used this country. It is, above all, an acceptance of equals. Xavier Herbert, who I later took to Lake Nash on the Queensland-Northern Territory border to revisit the scenes of *Capricornia*, said it all:

> Until we give back to the black man (sic) just a bit of the land that was his, and give it back without strings to snatch it back, without anything but generosity of spirit in concession for the evil that we have done to him – until we do that, we shall remain what we have always been so far, a people without integrity, not a nation but a community of thieves.

Our forebears who sailed from their homeland, as we did, in search of a better life and opportunities had also asked questions. Is there land freely available on which we can build security and a future for ourselves and our children? Can we overcome by force or moral rationalising those who are using the land now? If so, then our prosperity is assured, whatever short-term hardships we endure or crimes we commit in the name of necessity.

The point about these anecdotes is that they are not isolated exceptions, offcuts in an otherwise smooth construction of the inevitable coming of change. Together they have been welded to make a prison of our humanity. The reasons for the pain and guilt and anger and hope surrounding the Mabo debate lie in the suppression and distortions of the past, the cruelty, indifference, censorship and opportunities not taken. Confronted with such a history a great boil of Bosnian bitterness should be seething under every black skin. Yet such anger is rare.

At Yuendumu outside Alice Springs I interviewed an old man suffering from cancer but defying expectations of an early death by applying faith to his pain in the form of a tattered Bible pressed to his stomach when the pain intensified. He had been a child at the Coniston massacre in 1928 when pastoralists and miners killed men, women and children. He saw his relatives slaughtered. He remembered running into the bush while the horsemen rode around, shooting lead bullets into black bodies. Yet he was not bitter.

He was recruited by the army and worked on the road between Alice and Darwin. There he was bombed. He was then taken to New Guinea. A Japanese bullet creased his forehead. When demobbed he received no pension or other benefits, becoming one of the army's forgotten people.* Yet still he was not bitter.

Why was he behaving in so friendly a manner to me, freely sharing of his knowledge and history when my culture had treated him so shamefully? Why wasn't he outraged, demanding justice, cursing all? His answer was mild, forgiving: 'All right young fella. Some people make mistakes.'

The desk where I'm editing this book stands on land which was taken from its original owners, the Tjuat, by force. This happened before I was born, but not before the birth of my grandparents, though they never came to Australia. My family never pointed guns at those who lived here, Tacancut and his wife Tarkiena and their daughters Nhangaglian and Caeran; we have never erected fences to keep out Nogolgot, his wife Pategian and their son Tanhaglian, or the childless couple Caigoro and Adoron, all of whose bones now lie further north, at New Norcia, where Spanish monks provided the haven denied by the English invaders.

Though there is no blood on my hands or yours, you and I are the beneficiaries of our foreparents' actions or inactions. We are the recipients of stolen goods. The men who cleared the land of trees and rocks to grow crops and graze stock also cleared the land of its owners and users. Those invaders said they demolished and destroyed and killed for the sake of future generations. We are all part of that future planned by others. Like you, my family and I find shelter, warmth, profit, security, pleasure, comfort and joy from living on the proceeds of thieves and killers.

A kilometre beyond and below the computer screen is a large lake. On the old maps it's called Gabbia Yandirt, which is Noongar for fresh water. When George Moore, the colony's first

---

* Recognition of Aboriginal contribution to Australia's defence and proper payment of their services, largely the result of research by Major R.A. Hall, came too late for the black returned soldier. He died while we were still trying to organise a pension.

Attorney-General, rode up the Darling Range he asked those he encountered the name of the lake. They answered in practical terms, misunderstanding his question as he misinterpreted their reply, an encounter which enshrined in miniature the real story of Australia. Later maps call this Lake Chittering, derived from the onomatopoeic Noongar word 'chitty-chitty' for the willy wagtail which used to be common in this area. That was before a government campaign using residual chemicals against Argentine ants moved the insecticide up the food chain destroying birdlife. The ants had become a barbecue pest making outdoor entertaining a misery. This was an issue which had to be addressed.

The lake is no longer gabbia yandirt. It is polluted with phosphates from the fertilisers spread on the farms, then washed down with the topsoil from the cleared hills to clog the Brockman River. This creek is named after a 'pioneer settler' whose cruelty towards the Noongars last century shocked even his most heartless neighbours. In a paddock by the lake are said to lie the remnants of people who perished in the measles epidemic of last century, and who ran into the water to cool their burning bodies. A farmer recalls ploughing up the bones and throwing them into the fenceline, to the edge of cultivation, the fringe of productive industry. Had they been white bones the police would have been called. When questioned on time and place he grows cagey, fearing land claims and a black, red and yellow flag moving along the track towards his property, just as the union jack fluttered this way in my grandparents' lifetime.

Conservation and Land Management staff say chippings from stone tools have been found around the well which produces our water, but decline to produce the report, perhaps fearing more may be made of the findings. Down the road are riverside campsites known to have been used 40,000 years ago. Yet a consultants' report used by the Chittering Shire Council to justify further subdivision of the land mentions none of this, referring only to the fact that Aboriginal people 'frequented' the area, like birds and animals. Do whites 'frequent' Melbourne? Any further, more substantial, more human reference, would entail recognition of prior rights and the need for compensation.

A politician sneers when a reporter uses the term 'invasion', preferring his word 'colonisation'. This is the language which turns slaughter into ethnic cleansing. Is it no wonder then that we refuse to acknowledge the past and shrink from the questions it raises? Yet if these buried queries lie unconfronted and unanswered will they, like subterranean salt, seep to the surface to pollute relationships of the present and the future? Will they poison the land all must share if we are to avoid the divisions which have destroyed other societies?

Perhaps the answers could liberate.

9

OPPRESSION DOESN'T NEED ANOTHER RACE

Kim Beazley

The instructions to Captain James Cook from George III (first Voyage) were that he was to show the inhabitants of New Holland:

> ... every kind of civility and regard, and ... with their consent take possession of convenient situations in the country in the name of the King of Great Britian.

And the instructions of George III to Governor Philip regarding the Aboriginal inhabitants:

> To conciliate their affections, enjoining all our subjects to live in amity and kindness with them. And if any of our subjects shall wantonly destroy them, or give them an unnecessary interruption in their several occupations it is our will and pleasure that you do cause such offenders to be brought to punishment.

Early this century the anthropologist Roheim commented concerning Aborigines of the central Australian desert:

> Like every other human being he loves his home dearly. Their faces will brighten up when they speak of the place where they rata perama (become incarnated), or of other places of mythological fame, and they will call them tmarra knarra or

ngurru puntu – a big place. When one arrives at the big place in question, it is only a few trees and rocks, with perhaps a little water to account for its reputation. Yet Ltaltuma for the Aranda, or Ilpila for the Gumu has the same emotional value as London for an Englishman or Paris for a Frenchman.

When I was first elected to the House of Representatives in 1945, Aboriginal people and issues hardly featured in parliamentary records or debates. But I do remember the subject erupting as part of what we would now call 'the cold war.' Dr Herbert Evatt (former Attorney-General in the Curtin Government, later president of the General Assembly of the United Nations [UN]) at one time in the UN raised the question of human rights in the Soviet Union.

After an attack by John Beasley, envoy to the UN as temporary Australian delegate, Mikhail Molotov, the Soviet foreign minister, counter-attacked with stories of human rights abuses in Australia. Photographs of Aboriginal people in police custody in Western Australia were shown in the UN General Assembly. The prisoners were chained to one another by the neck, and wore leg chains when being led to some process of what passed for 'justice' in Western Australia.

In the UN at that early stage, race issues did not have the large audience of sympathetic voting delegates as later when many former black African colonies became members of the world body.

Until the 1967 referendum the Constitution prohibited the Commonwealth from legislating for Aboriginal people, but in the UN no one was interested in attributing defects in policy to the States. Constitutional niceties about the Commonwealth only being responsible in the Northern Territory cut no ice with Africa and the Soviet Bloc. Anything done adversely to Aboriginal people was attributed to Australia.

In the 1950s I attended a conference of Moral Rearmament (MRA) at Caux in Switzerland. MRA was then battling to bring sanity to a demoralised Europe. The discipline of MRA is to follow an enlightened conscience without self-interest or dishonesty and to concentrate on situations in the world requiring restitution and reconciliation.

Racial oppression had been a leading feature of Europe. If you follow a discipline of the conscience you cannot simply point the finger at other nations and individuals. The moral Achilles heel of Australia was the position of Aboriginal people, their poverty, ill health and powerlessness. The Achilles heel of Kim Beazley was that he had not really concerned himself about Aboriginal people, or made friendship with them, or listened to them. This led to a U-turn in my life.

My first thoughts were: if Aboriginal people are acknowledged to own land they will negotiate from a position of strength. If they do not they'll be in a position of weakness.

Early in the 1950s at the Adelaide Conference of the Australian Labor Party I successfully moved that the platform should acknowledge that Aboriginal people owned land, and what was meant was tribal land. It could apply immediately only in Commonwealth territories if Labor was in power. The idea didn't get widespread support; Jock Nelson, the member for the Northern Territory, didn't think it a vote winner.

Well into the 1960s neither Gordon Bryant (who was to become the first Minister for Aboriginal Affairs in the Whitlam Government) nor I had any conception that the British believed that there was 'terra nullius'. Governor Arthur Phillip was instructed not to interfere with the land ownership of the natives. Cook had described the people and in his log commented that their happiness was greater than that of Europeans. I do not know how academics and lawyers derived the theory of 'terra nullius' if that means that 'there was nobody there'.

Of course what subsequently happened in Australia was exactly how the Crown (that is, the group which commanded Parliament, the courts, the armed services, the ministry) had treated the Irish, and their own lower orders.

This exercise of power in Ireland was conquest. The land of the Irish was mostly seized, and settled ('the plantation'). All the 'sacred sites' of the Irish were confiscated – every cathedral, abbey, priory, seminary and parish church was handed over to a body called the 'Church of Ireland' to which only about 8 per cent of the people belonged. Everybody was required to pay a tenth of their income (the tithe) to the Church of Ireland.

John Hunter, the second Governor of New South Wales (described by Manning Clark as a man of 'incorruptible integrity, unceasing zeal and a sound and impartial judgment'), received a fleet of Irish prisoners with no list of their names or details of their crimes. He protested to the Secretary of State for the Colonies. He was told that he could not be informed who they were, or what they had done.

There had been resistance to the payment of the tithe in many parts of Ireland. Hessian and Hanoverian troops of His Majesty, who spoke no English, had rounded up whole villages and put them on the ships. Many may well have actually paid the tithe. But do not send them back! Imperial policy in Ireland was to take the land and the culture. They had no right to be Catholics, to have Catholic religious orders or schools or Catholic properties.

For long periods the Irish, who were allowed to be tenants on what was once their land, had no recourse but to humour. There were degrees of liberation but never the return of land or sacred sites.

What happened to Aboriginal people slowly (it took forty years to cross the Blue Mountains) happened swiftly to the Irish. If you can call Aboriginal and Irish experience 'racism' you must call what happened to English and Scottish lower orders 'classism.'

There had been traditional rights of occupation and cultivation of common land. The nobility and gentry sat in Parliament and passed thousands of Enclosure Acts, expelling the people who had worked the land and where they'd derived their livelihood. As far as ownership was concerned it was 'terra nullius' though not called that. The Scottish did not use the polite term 'enclosure'. They called it 'the clearances'.

What I am trying to say is that what happened to Aboriginal people was par for the course of those times. One million Irish starved to death in the 'Great Hunger' of the 1840s while the

United Kingdom Parliament dithered as to whether or not to repeal the Corn Laws and import food.

Perhaps it was all this which led Prime Minister Paul Keating to say that he called for:

an act of recognition that it was WE who did the depossessing. WE took the traditional way of life. WE brought the diseases and alcohol. WE committed the murders. WE took the children from their mothers. WE practised discrimination and exclusion. It was OUR ignorance and OUR prejudice. With some noble exceptions we failed to make the most basic human response and enter into their hearts and minds. We failed to ask: How would I feel if this were done to me. As a consequence we failed to see that what we were doing degraded all of us.

Perhaps a person with an Irish background could see all this with greater clarity than most of us.

In the first days of European settlement an Aboriginal leader known as Yagan was strolling near the rudimentary town of Perth when he came upon a military flogging of a soldier. In those days flogging was almost a mania in the British Army and Navy; many early settlers were Waterloo veterans and accepted this as a matter of course.

The floggings often exposed the spine and Yagan saw one which did. He protested, screaming and waving his hands with horror. This was deadly. This reaction treated whites as barbarians and obviously implied that he was too civilised for the European barbarians, which of course he was. He became a marked man. He was shot and his head sent to England for the 'scientific' idiots of the time.

(At the 1992 Caux conference of the MRA May O'Brien, the recently retired superintendent of Aboriginal education in Western Australia raised with the English people present the fact that there was a great collection of Aboriginal skulls in Britain. She said the return of the skulls to proper burial in Australia related to the peace of the souls of Aboriginal people past and present.)

The first Anglican Bishop of Perth was Matthew Hale who had been associated with Aboriginal protection in South Australia. He came to a European community which regarded itself as a civilising force among barbarians. Any challenge to this concept was resented.

Bishop Hale ran into the same hostility as Yagan. In his church journal he criticised the cruelties. Steadily his position became untenable. He eventually had to return to England. Largely as a consequence of the work of William Wilberforce there existed in Britain anti-slavery and Aboriginal protection societies. What Hale had to say and write began to cause concern. In the nineteenth century an Anglican bishop was somebody, and if he spoke on an obviously Christian humanitarian issue it had social influence.

The Parliament of the United Kingdom drafted a constitution for Western Australia which came into force in 1889. It provided for an obligatory allocation out of the colonial budgets for Aboriginal welfare and left no doubt that Aboriginal people were British subjects, a somewhat mystic status implying the right to some protection.

Indians in Canada were 'British subjects'. The Royal Canadian Mounted Police were controlled from London till 1867, and from Ottawa thereafter. If you murdered an Indian you were hanged exactly as if you'd killed any other British subject. It was a misfortune of Aborigines that Western Australian police were not controlled from London. As for the budget provision for their welfare, the colonial Parliament of Western Australia in 1904 (now the State Parliament) legislated to repeal this irksome guaranteed expenditure.

The State Governor, believing it to be an entrenched clause of the Constitution derived from imperial authority, vetoed it for imperial scrutiny. Unluckily for the Aborigines the Secretary of State for the Colonies in 1904 was Joseph Chamberlain. He had worked for war in South Africa to assert the rights of British settlers and gold companies in the Transvaal and the Orange Free State. The Boer War was his achievement. He simply said he claimed no jurisdiction on this issue in Western Australia, and Aboriginal people were abandoned.

Over the years I made friends. Gallurwuy Yunupingu and Wulaymbuma Wunungmurra I accompanied to the Caux conference and Irwin Lewis to the United States. I got to know Harold Blair, a fine singer, the Roberts family in the Northern Territory (see Douglas Lockwood's book *I the Aboriginal*), Douglas Nicholls, later to become Governor of South Australia – Aborigines who thought systematically about the position of their people. I also came to know the people of Yirrkala (on the north-east of Arnhem Land).

They had lived for some years on a mission reserve but from time immemorial in the same area. Vital land was to be taken from this country for a foreign company, Pechiney, to take bauxite. Bauxite mining sweeps the surface of the land, creating a moonscape. The people were alarmed and Gordon Bryant and I went to see them. They revealed sacred and secret sacred sites, and pointed out that mining effluent channelled into Melville Bay would destroy the fishing.

I wrote to Mission Superintendent Edgar Wells in 1963, and thirty years later I still believe my words then to be the issue today:

> The problem is one for the Parliament and the issue it poses is this: Is the Aboriginal Australian an Australian citizen, or is he one of a conquered people? If he is an Australian citizen he rightly asks the Australian Parliament to consult him before dispossession. If Aborigines are a conquered people no consultation is necessary. As a corollary, their proper course of action is an appeal to the UN, not Parliament.

But the first step was a petition to Parliament. Edgar Wells records its origin from his point of view:

After breakfast one morning I found the two men [Gordon Bryant and myself] in [the mission] church; they were engaged in a serious religious conversation and eventually it involved discussion about the freshly painted Aboriginal art boards and what they meant within the Aboriginal cultural system.

These paintings were of superb quality. The artist had been fascinated by the New Testament story of tongues of fire resting on the heads of the believers at Pentecost, and the theme of inspiration. Edgar Wells wrote:

> It was here in the sanctuary that Mr Kim Beazley had what he afterwards described as a 'guided' inspiration concerning a petition to Canberra ... 'Make a bark petition,' he later advised his Aboriginal friends, 'a petition surrounded with an Aboriginal painting will be irresistible.' And it proved to be so.*

The petition stirred a press furore and the House of Representatives sent an all-party committee to hear the grievances of the Yirrkala people. The committee recommended Aboriginal land ownership, the first time, I suspect, in Australian history. The principle was established but it would be fair to say that nobody envisaged the tracts of land in the Northern Territory and South Australia which were acknowledged as being Aboriginal freehold and which cover an area about the size of New South Wales. Although difficult to realise now, most of it (apart from South Australia) was initiated by the Liberal Government of Malcolm Fraser with Fred Chaney as Minister for Aboriginal Affairs, after initial moves by the Whitlam Government.

When I became Minister for Education I was driven by two convictions. The first was that to deny a people an education in their own language was to treat them as a conquered people, and

---

* For more details of the Yirrkala petition see Edgar Wells' *Reward and Punishment in Arnhem Land*.

we have always treated Aborigines as a conquered people. When the Whitlam Government fell in 1975 there were schools teaching in twenty-two Aboriginal languages. The valid educational point is that literacy in a second language (English) is the more readily established if it has first been established in the mother tongue – the language of the heart.

My second conviction was that if a student is Aboriginal, then the chances are high that the child, and his or her family, are poor. Hence every Aboriginal child in secondary education was put on what amounts to a scholarship.

I no longer believe that there is a wonderful world conscience out there judging us by our policies on race relations. I wish there were. The Soviet Union, once a major critic, has stopped lying about the way it treated Poles (Katyn), the racial minorities deported to Siberia. The butchery in Uganda, Siberia, Ruanda, Burundi, Angola, Mozambique, Ethiopia, Eritrea and elsewhere has destroyed the moral authority of large parts of Africa to be critical of policies and attitudes in Australia.

The events in Iraq, Turkey, the former Yugoslavia and Somalia all parade the same tragedy of 'racism'. As in so much of history, oppression does not need a different race to thrive.

Robert Tickner, the present Federal Minister for Aboriginal Affairs shocked me by quoting something I said twenty-five years ago:

I say that the Australian people must be deliberately responsible. I believe their very security is involved in their being able to say to the world that this community will ensure sane and just race relations.

I don't know about the world observing but God is observing. The Keating statement contains what theologians would call Repentance, Restitution and Reconciliation. The secular world will probably not accept this interpretation. But in our race relations they are the essential steps for a better future where we can all live together in mutual respect.

10

PORTRAIT OF THE HISTORIAN AS A YOUNG LEARNER

Geoffrey Bolton

Growing up in Perth in the 1930s and 1940s I can't remember meeting any Aborigines. I must have seen them during visits to the country, in Pingelly, Narrogin, or Wickepin, but they have left no impression on my conscious memory.

Not that my experience was unusual. Since 1928 Aborigines had been prohibited from coming into the central parts of Perth and Fremantle. I believe that some Aboriginal men used to make a living hawking clothes-props around the suburbs, but they never came to our backyard. There was an Aboriginal camp at the back of Bassendean, and another at the end of Devon Road in Swanbourne – at least there was until a neighbouring householder complained, and the Nedlands council razed it with a bulldozer. But these were both well out of the way, and in any case it was doubtful if white visitors were allowed without a permit. By the time I went to university in 1948 I knew a fair bit about Aborigines from reading and absolutely nothing at first hand.

Consciousness was raised a little at The University of Western Australia. Two of my ex-servicemen friends, Les Marchant and George Paquin, were cadet patrol officers with the Department of Native Affairs, and Les once enlivened a rather grand Sunday morning drinks party by bringing along samples of the department's plug tobacco for some of us to chew, to the great detriment of a bed of lobelias on which we soon ejected. David Hutchison took me out to the Bassendean camp to meet the inhabitants, but I didn't know what to say to them, and I couldn't understand much of what they were saying, and I felt embarrassed by the poverty and the dejection. So I never followed up the visit.

A city boy all my life – if Perth in that period qualified as a city – I thought it my duty as a good Australian to become acquainted with the outback. Having none of the skills to make myself useful on a cattle station, I had to use my craft as a novice historian. After writing my honours thesis on Alexander Forrest, explorer and namer of the Kimberleys, I decided to write my Master of Arts on the history of the Kimberley pastoral industry. My resourceful professor, Fred Alexander, found me 100 pounds for fieldwork, solemnly warned me against even thinking of spending a penny more, and encouraged me to stay away as long as possible.

I set out in the third week of June 1952 after promising my parents that I would write regularly to them, and so unconsciously providing the source material for the rest of this essay. After taking the train to Meekatharra, I rode the mail-truck along the inland road through Peak Hill and Nullagine, and arrived in Marble Bar with a day to spare.

Here, according to my first letter:

> I yarned with several of the local inhabitants, including the local police officer, who presented me with some sample tin crushings, and a notorious character named Don McLeod who was, and perhaps still is, a communist, and who has induced all the natives working on the neighbouring stations to quit work, and to come in on a cooperative tin and wolfram mine which he has started.
>
> I met the man, who lives in a camp no better than a native camp, wearing a beard and shorts, and I think he's quite sincere, and a persuasive talker, but his enthusiasm is causing him to bite off more than he can chew, and if, as seems likely, the scheme should end in a fiasco, the repercussions will be heard in Perth, which so far seems to have been complacently ignoring the whole episode. McLeod is not altogether without

justification, as the natives haven't been treated uniformly well on the stations, and hence responded to any prospect of improvement such as he offers them. I also met the local MLA, Rodoreda, a friendly but rather ordinary sort of bloke.

Oh dear. I was a smug young bourgeois: and indeed a hypocrite. The truth was that McLeod and his offsider, Don Stuart (later author of *Yandy* and in time a friend), impressed me considerably. I was severely editing the truth so as not to shock my parents. I couldn't help noticing that the Aboriginal people in McLeod's camp were easier and more direct to talk to. They clearly knew what they were doing as they went about their work yandying alluvial in the creek beds. And McLeod was one of those people to whom the overworked word 'charisma' might fairly be applied. All the same, my doubts were justified by the over-confidence with which he spoke of his ability to deal with financiers in Adelaide and Sydney. Within a year or two they got the better of him.

I moved on to Broome and then, for the next five weeks stayed at various Kimberley pastoral properties. It was clear that on cattle stations Aboriginal people were an essential part of the workforce. Their relations with their employers reminded me a little of what I'd read of the Roman villa and the Norman feudal system. The Aboriginal workers were ill paid, and still on some Kimberley properties not paid at all; but their families were fed, they had access to the Flying Doctor service and the Australian Inland Mission hospitals, and the bosses had no interest in interfering with their cultural practices.

I saw no brutality, nor heard boast of it. But I couldn't help remembering an anecdote McLeod had told me of two veteran Kimberley pastoralists yarning around the campfire, one of them saying, as was so often said: 'It's no use paying the coons, they don't know the value of money', and the other replying, 'And we'll take bloody good care they never find out!' But I had very little direct conversation with the Aborigines. I was diffident, and deplorably unaware of the value of Aboriginal informants about the past. That was until the manager of Noonkanbah introduced me to one veteran who could remember the Fitzroy valley hostilities of the 1890s: 'Bin shoot'em, shoot'em all the morning'. In those days young historians were not alerted to the value of oral history.

At the end of July I made my headquarters for a while at Moola Bulla, then the government-owned cattle station for Aborigines.* The manager, Lew McBeath, had taken over in 1949 from a predecessor who had left under a cloud. I never found out the details, but there was said to have been cattle duffing, and his treatment of the Aborigines had been suspect. As I read the station journals, I wondered what lay behind the entry for 11 October 1946:

> William William, Lamarer, Tommy King, Jacky Perris caused trouble with another Halls Creek boy for no reason and influenced others to cause trouble, left their work and came in to station, where they were duly put in chains and returned.

'In chains'; and this was only six years before my visit, not at some remote era of the pioneering frontier. McBeath in my view was doing an excellent job within the paternalist traditions of the time. I quote again from my letters home:

> The schoolteachers ... are both retired teachers who were re-employed by the Education Department when they came up here to tutor the Aboriginal children. They have only been on the job for two years, but what they have done is pretty impressive, as the kids, most of whom had no previous tuition, can now read second and third standard literature, and have grasped the important bits of arithmetic such as multiplication, division, addition and subtraction. When you compare this to what the average kid learns in two years it is pretty

---

* Moola Bulla was an Aboriginal reserve from 1910 to 1954 when it was sold by the Western Australian Government to non-Aboriginal graziers.

favourable, and would seem to dispel any idea that the native kid is, in actual aptitude, much inferior to the white.

The reason why the native kids fail to develop on a par with the whites may be seen in the conditions in which they live out of school. You couldn't give a black child homework, or encourage them to do any extra reading, when most of them live in a camp with several other families of all ages, and the home conditions are just nonexistent. What is holding down the native kids is the fact that they are living with their elders, who are set in their ways, and like most people, don't like to see their offspring get too much above them, or away from the old influences. The answer to this problem seems to be well-run boarding schools.

Still the young paternalist, I was at least learning about Aboriginal capacity. Moola Bulla gave its inhabitants more than formal education. A public health inspector was running a hygiene school at which Aboriginal people from across the Kimberley were shown recent advances in waste disposal and sanitation. Houses were built for several of the Moola Bulla stockmen and their families. Twice a week there was an openair film show, which attracted visitors from Halls Creek, 25 kilometres distant, but the Moola Bulla Aboriginal people were the main audience.

On other nights there was community singing. Country and western ballads such as 'The Dear Old Aussie Blues' and 'When the Rain Tumbles Down in July' gained an extra potency from being modulated with the half-tones and rhythms of Aboriginal singing. There were also plenty of sporting events. I have never been an athlete, but I was encouraged to play basketball with the Aborigines, only to find to my chagrin that they soon realised I was a poor player and took care to feed me my share of the ball. This contrasted with the aggressive competitiveness that I usually found in team sports.

From Moola Bulla I visited several neighbouring properties, including the stations owned by the large absentee British firm,

Vesteys:

> ... at Gordon Downs the staff seemed to be in the grip of alcoholic paralysis; there was a handyman who had been a British colonel as recently as the second world war; an unmarried governess, five months pregnant, and no gentlewoman; a young bookkeeper about my own age who was planning to get out of the place as soon as possible, and who broke the bad news to me that although they'd had piles of records going back at least as far as 1903, they had carefully and painstakingly burnt the lot last year; the manager, who regarded himself as a caretaker ... and the manager's wife, amiable, but also a little tipsy, as well as a couple of unrestrained kids, alternatively spoiled and screamed at. The sort of place it is, they empty their nightsoil pans on the open ground only about a hundred yards from the house ...

The public health inspector who had found the Aborigines so ready to learn the techniques of hygienic sanitation was scathing in his report on Gordon Downs. As I told my parents:

> Moola Bulla, where nearly all the work is done by natives and halfcastes, sets a standard of efficiency which only points the contrast to these other places ... But all the natives look remarkably happy ... and many of them are quite handy tradesmen. One cut my hair on Friday, didn't do a bad job either for an amateur.

It was too good to last. By paying the stockmen better wages than the neighbouring properties, and by providing conditions which showed up the parsimony of the big absentee companies, McBeath aroused antagonism among many of the East Kimberley pastoralists. He was on the wrong side in some office politics at the Department of Native Affairs, and when allegations of ill treatment were levelled against McBeath and his staff the State Government decided to close Moola Bulla. In 1955 the property was sold to a Queenslander who promptly ousted all the Aboriginal inhabitants to become fringedwellers at Halls Creek and Fitzroy Crossing, and then boasted to the media about the bargain he had made in acquiring the station for far less than its value.

But Moola Bulla had taken the crude edges off my ignorant prejudices. I returned from the Kimberley convinced of the need to free Aborigines from their legal restrictions, and had written my first letter to the *West Australian* on the subject before the end of the year. I still had a long way to go, but I had learned respect for Aboriginal capacity.

11

SEARCHING FOR A BLACK ANCESTRY

Robert Juniper

My first experience with Aboriginal people was a very vivid one, and a lasting memory. My parents took me to a corroboree near Merredin when I was about five years old (c. 1934). I can still see the sparks flying into the black sky and the tall glistening men stomping and raising the red dust in clouds. I recently spoke to my mother about it. She remembers the occasion very well.

We walked to the site, my younger brother in a pram. It was not advertised, the word was passed around. Mum is adamant that there were no local Aboriginal people involved and thinks it must have been a gathering of various groups from around the district. The show was not put on for whites, though it certainly was a curio. Yet at the same time I am sure the whites had no idea of anything significant except for the spectacle, which left an indelible impression on me. I imagine it was a privilege to attend as I do not know of anyone else besides my Aboriginal friends who has been to a corroboree so long ago.

I do not recall seeing Aboriginal people as a presence in Merredin as I did in Kalgoorlie. For a short time in my childhood I also lived in Kal. We saw Aboriginal people all the time – the urban fringe dwellers selling clothesline props and often begging, using the following little rhyme:

Gib-it sugar, gib-it tea,
Gib-it flour for pickaninny.

There were also the half-naked men with spears – straight off the desert. I remember being, if not afraid, then slightly apprehensive at their presence; probably learned from the attitude of my parents and grandparents. The 'stranger danger' threat was prevalent then too, it seems.

I am sure that blacks and whites were not any closer in those days; quite the contrary. 'They' were looked on as a sort of alien race from both sides, and my family then did not have any relationship with the Aborigines as I and my family do now, working, living, socialising. I can honestly say I never heard any racist reference in my home except for my father's hatred of the Germans. In fact my mother always spoke of Aboriginal people with a sort of awe and pride: 'Some are so black charcoal would make a light mark on them', I once heard her say. And when I did eventually make contact with Aboriginal people there was, and still is, a shyness – both ways. I suppose I could generalise and say that this is what can be misconstrued by both sides as aloofness or antagonism, leading to misunderstandings which form the basis for a lot of what is considered racism.

All this was in the early 1930s – for we went to England just before the war, and I returned in 1947, when I was in my late teens; a young man whose recent experiences were of the English countryside. So when I began painting, it was in the English modern mode. I had yet to see the Australian landscape destined to move me. That was not to happen for a few more years.

It came about when I visited the sheep station managed by my younger brother, Ted. There I really met Aboriginal people for the first time. Gibson Desert people, who had never seen the ocean or a city and thought the images of the Milky Way and the moon as seen through my astronomical telescope were tricks inside the instrument. I had no way of explaining magnification to them because I did not have any of their language, and they only had minimal pieces of mine.

This encounter with the Aboriginal people and the stunning revelation of the desert landscape were pivotal for my painting. I had absorbed the European influences into a personal approach to Australian landscape. I considered it inappropriate not to make reference to the original inhabitants.

I started painting the landscape, distressed by the recent arrivals who took what they wanted and then departed, leaving the detritus of their works and lifestyle, showing the same disdain for the land as they had for the Aborigines. So I painted figures as small markers, lost, dispossessed, generally walking away in the distance, symbolic of our alienation of them in their own place, blowing across the landscape like litter and treated by most with about equal respect.

My paintings often have an aerial view, as I have flown over the country in light aircraft. I also find it desirable to make overland excursions to the desert areas to get a sense of place for my paintings. I do not paint exact reproductions of the landscape. My work is more an emotional reaction to the site and its history, though there are references to some recognisable elements which people who know the areas can identify.

I find I have a knack of locating what seem to be Aboriginal sacred sites, and have a good collection of grinding stones found in various long abandoned spots, and which I'm sure many people have passed by without noticing. Finding sites seems to me to be largely a matter of observation and commonsense. I look for an outstanding feature, high rocks, caves, sheltered places, arranged stones, rock shards that do not belong to that particular place – often near to waterholes or places where the group would have easy access to water or food.

While there is no formal acknowledgment of Aboriginal 'blood' in my family, there are several anecdotes relating to chance comments made to ancestors and even young people in other branches of the family today, showing that they have been mistaken for people of Aboriginal descent. I have a fair skin, yet in a pub in Sydney once was called over to a group of Aboriginal people on the other side of the room because they felt they needed to clear up whether there was any black 'blood' in me. When I said to one, 'My grandmother was darker than you', he said to his mates, 'What did I tell you?'

I'm currently researching my ancestry, and find that a great-great-grandfather has no recorded birth date, though his place of birth was recorded in the death certificate as New South Wales. This is the first major evidence to convince me that he was Aboriginal, because Aboriginal births were not considered important enough to be recorded until fairly recent times.

Forty years ago Sidney Nolan remarked: 'When you consider white history in Australia you should look to the Irish: if you consider the future you must look to the Aborigines.' A statement that would have brought a smirk to the faces of most whites at that time – people who'd had minimal or no contact with Aboriginal people, and certainly no social interaction with them.

These people now have to come to terms with the fact that the law has at last recognised that this country was originally occupied by the Aborigines, who are now beginning to find a voice that is being heard, and, through our laws, starting to get initial responses to some of their claims. The white Australians must start recognising that the rent for their recent tenancy is well overdue.

An American visitor to these shores about thirty years ago remarked to me, 'We have trouble with our blacks, you just ignore yours.' Yet that comment glosses over the way the Aborigines were really treated, and the fact that they have much to be angry about. I said to my friend Stephen 'Baamba' Albert on a trip to Lombadina: 'We are lucky that you guys don't have the same animosity that the blacks in the States have', for I feel that we richly deserve some reaction to the actions and attitudes of our forebears, and to what is happening now.

Baamba agreed, and said, 'We have no anger or animosity at all.' And I imagine that goes for most of the Aboriginal communities in the country as opposed to the urban fringe-dwellers whose lives are so different, and who are still treated as so much refuse.

Yet I know this is simplistic, for in my short experience I have heard resentment from the older people when it comes to matters of their past. One woman spoke heatedly about how she had no intention of cooperating with researchers trying to compile a dictionary of her language, for she still burned at the inequity of not being allowed to speak her own tongue at school when she was a little girl living in a Catholic mission.

And while I know it is not done to be racist in public now, much like picking your nose should not be done in public but is condoned in private, I imagine racism is not far below the surface for most non-Aboriginal Australians. One only has to look at joke-telling to get a sense of this. One hears jokes about Irishmen, Polish or the South African Van der Merwe, or Dad and Dave in Australia. Generally they are bland or, if not, people tell them to their friends of that nationality and everyone enjoys the laugh, each pulling out a joke against each other's original homeland.

But jokes about Aborigines are cruel and hateful, even destructively exterminatory, and evoke gales of mirth, hardly ever tinged with guilt. And you don't see the whites sharing these jokes with the blacks. The other joke topics that cause similar reactions are those about AIDS and feminists or dumb women, and these too seem to be coming from a base of insecurity and antagonism against the threat from outside.

It is only a matter of a few years since the indigenous people, dispossessed and treated like untouchables, have had the legal right of access to similar day-to-day privileges other Australians take for granted. It is only thirty years ago that you were likely to be arrested if you took an Aboriginal person into a posh restaurant. And while there are laws requiring equal opportunity for all Australian citizens, custom still enforces many of the poor practices of the past.

And this is impacting on me to a slight degree today. There is something not quite acceptable to some of my contemporaries in searching for one's 'black' ancestry. Since I have started featuring Aboriginal figures large in my work, and since I have been painting works highlighting the differences between white and black, I notice that some of my more urbane contemporaries are slightly more supercilious and bland about my work than they used to be about my pure landscapes. Apparently they felt these earlier works were particularly important in the history of Australian art. It seems that these later works are slightly embarrassing, and there is some doubt about their importance as art. I believe this reaction is more to do with a manifestation of subtle prejudice than a comment on my talents as an artist. Time will tell.

12

THE PRESENCE WHICH IS ABSENCE

Veronica Brady

It's a kind of presence, I suppose. It comes out of an awareness going back to the childhood of something, someone, some people, who have been here before me, have had some effect on, and still have some kind of power over me. They make demands which I do not understand but obscurely know that I must respond to and honour.

The first time I was conscious of Aboriginal Australians was as a child, quite small. I was wandering on my own towards a group of people who interested me, when my mother called me back. It was on the banks of the Murray, probably around about Mildura. I must have seen an Aboriginal camp and wanted to explore these people who looked so different and lived so differently from any I had met so far. All I remember is my mother calling: 'Come back, darling. They're Aborigines' (or was it 'blacks'?).

I don't remember anything else; what I saw, or what, if anything, these Aboriginal people said or did, whether they were welcoming or turned away. I recall only my mother's words. As I remember them, there was no hostility. Nothing to make me frightened. Just a sense that between us and them there was a kind of gap.

They were not people who belonged to our world, nor did I belong to theirs. Somehow, it seemed, we were not the same kind of people. But there was nothing frightening or evil about them as I recall, only something strange which had apparently interested me and which I wanted to explore.

Looking back I do not think my parents were hostile either. They were both educated and remarkably open-minded about other people and cultures and they raised us also to be open-minded and tolerant. But this was the late 1930s when Aboriginal people figured little in anyone's consciousness. When anyone did have a view it was that they were 'dying out', 'Stone-age people' unfortunately unable to cope with the impact of 'civilisation'. Their fate was either to learn to become like us or disappear.

In Victoria, those who survived were invisible. I should think my encounter by the Murray was the first time I'd even seen an Aboriginal person, though I do have an obscure memory (which may be imaginary) of a black man hanging around the yard of one of the hotels in St Arnaud on the edge of the Mallee where we lived for a time.

True, we read about them occasionally, the 'innocent children of nature' of *We Of The Never Never* (by Mrs Aeneas Gunn) and I was especially fascinated by the necklaces of fleas which Bett-Bett would make. I loved the image of the little black girl – a princess – sitting in the dust like a particularly impish mascot, but admired the heroic pioneering woman whose story the book really told.

That was the stuff of imperial fantasy, of course, though in this case it was benevolent enough. It also produced the figure of the 'little black boy' (always a boy and always African). We gave some of our pocket money to help the missionaries 'convert' him to Christianity, putting our pennies into what we called the 'Jackie mite box'. Today I see this was the product of a larger fantasy of 'race' and racial superiority, part of what one scholar has called the Manichean* allegory which underlay – and still underlies – the Western claim to dominate the world and assumes that 'white' is to 'black' as good to evil, civilised to savage, superior to inferior, adult to child, rational to irrational, and so on.

---

* Belief that the material world is an invasion of goodness by the powers of evil and that Satan was co-eternal with God.

I think this was the case for my parents even though they, my father particularly, had little time for notions of Empire, Being both of Irish descent. As a young man my father had refused to fight in the First World War, seeing no point in defending the British Empire. His sympathies were with the victims of power rather than with the powerful. He voted Labor, supported the union movement and taught us to sympathise with the Jewish refugees who came to Australia from Hitler's Germany in the late 1930s.

He must also have had some feeling for Aboriginal people because he introduced us to Frank Dalby Davidson's *Children of the Dark People*, is a novel about two Aboriginal children separated from the rest of their tribe by an earthquake which raised a mountain range between them and the others. It takes the children, their culture and adventures seriously and it introduced me for the first time to an ancient culture and its richness.

But this was only one book. Like most Australians of that time, and Roman Catholics especially, I grew up looking to Europe, listening to my father's stories of his travels there and in the United States of America, reading mostly English stories and learning about European history.

True, we were also raised to be self-consciously Australian. Until I was about nine or ten we lived in the country, in Seymour first and then St Arnaud. My father loved the bush. We would go bush-walking, especially in spring when the wildflowers were in bloom. Or we would explore by car through the Mallee, up to the Murray and into the Riverina or, our special favourite, to the Grampians, twin mountain ranges thrust up from the plains of the Wimmera.

One part called 'Wonderland' because of its spectacular rock formations was our special favourite. Looking back, I realise it must have been a very special place also for its Aboriginal inhabitants, and today there is an Aboriginal Centre and museum nearby. However, in those days there was no sense of this past and certainly no sense of our being intruders.

The Australia I inhabited was discovered by Captain Cook,

founded by Captain Phillip and expressed for me by Henry Lawson and Banjo Paterson (both of whom my father admired). Later as an undergraduate I discovered writers like Eleanor Dark, Barnard Eldershaw and Katharine Susannah Prichard and, amongst the poets, Francis Webb, Rosemary Dobson and Judith Wright.

It's only in the last decade since I came to live in Western Australia that I've come to be more fully aware of the Aboriginal presence and of Aboriginal culture as something still living today. I've also learned more of the grim story of our relations with the indigenous people, which the frenzy over Mabo suggests is not yet over. In Western Australia Aboriginal people are still visible even in the city and on the edges of country towns in the settled areas and especially in the North-West where they are still a sizeable part of the population.

Since most of the State is unsuitable for our kind of stock and grain farming the land is still lightly settled, much of it 'desert' to our eyes. So proportionally more Aboriginal people have survived here than elsewhere, many of them living still on or near their original country – hence the agitation the Mabo decision has caused some Western Australians. The frontier days have not yet passed in Western Australia.

I first became aware of this during the Noonkanbah dispute. Before that my interest had been academic, arising out of my interest in Australian literature and history. I had not troubled myself much about specifically Aboriginal issues. True, I was interested in Aboriginal culture and had come across the poems of Oodgeroo Noonuccal (at that time known as Kath Walker) and the early plays of Jack Davis. I had also come in contact with the New Era Aboriginal Fellowship and knew one or two people who worked there, helping Aboriginal people settle into jobs and into suburban living. But it was all fairly distant.

At the same time I thought of myself as 'progressive' and opposed to racism. As a graduate student in North America in the 1960s I had been very self-righteous in my criticism of the way Americans treated black people, and I still remember how surprised I was when, in the middle of a discussion about the civil rights movement, someone retorted that as an Australian I had no right to be critical and that our Aboriginal people were even worse treated. That shock didn't last long and my attention was soon taken with other matters, the Vietnam war, opposition to nuclear power and uranium mining, the women's movement and so on.

Then in 1979 the mining company, Amax, applied for permission to prospect for oil on Noonkanbah station, one of the few in those days run by Aboriginal people. Amax wanted to drill on a sacred site and the Aborigines refused. At this the Premier Sir Charles Court threw the resources of the State on the company's side, providing a police escort for the drilling trucks. The convoy drove more than 1,500 kilometres to force its way onto the site against the opposition of the Aboriginal people and their supporters. The hole was drilled, but the well was dry.

In the controversy over the affair I began to realise that many, perhaps most, Western Australians did not know what the word 'sacred' meant. For them land was merely an economic proposition. The Aboriginal people, they argued, had forfeited rights to the land because they had failed to 'develop' the land, to use it to make money. It was not only preposterous, they thought, but also wrong, to stand in the way of those who wished to exploit the earth and its resources.

I also began to realise how devoted most Western Australians were to neo-Darwinism ideas of struggle and 'survival of the fittest'. In their view Aboriginal people were 'primitive', unable to cope with 'civilisation' – our culture of consumption and material productivity. Therefore they were 'doomed' they said, to giveway before the onward march of 'progress' and would probably die out. Some people also implied or argued that the notion that there was something special about a few unusual-looking rocks in the desert was ridiculous, mere primitive superstition; what was really valuable was money.

I had been raised as a Roman Catholic with a sense of the sacred, of some power beyond our rational comprehension or control, before whom or which we ought to bow down in reverence and with a kind of awe. So I could understand that a place might be holy, a place where this power was especially present and made special demands.

I also began to realise that many people did not share this sense, and that they and I did not really agree on what was valuable and worthwhile. The Aboriginal people of Noonkanbah were prepared to stand up to vast pressure from the government and mining companies with their international connections and resourses on behalf of what they held sacred.

Another incident around the same time clinched the matter for me. It was a hot summer night, and I had been invited to attend a meeting at a community hall in the Swan Valley. A group of middle-class Aboriginal people had moved into this area, bought houses and hoped to settle down. Their neighbours, mostly newly arrived migrants and, judging by their voices, from the north of England, were hostile. Land values would fall, they said, if 'blacks' moved in. There had been a series of incidents. Fights between Aboriginal and non-Aboriginal children at school and on school buses, rubbish dumped on lawns, trading of insults and arguments. So the Aboriginal people had called a public meeting to ask their non-Aboriginal neighbours what they had to do to be accepted.

I listened and watched the Aborigines who had to listen as the whites expressed their contempt and disgust, running through the lexicon of prejudices, calling Aborigines dirty, feckless, drunken troublemakers, anti-social, and so on and so forth. Sensing the fear as well as hatred in their voices, the fear of the unknown and fear of losing money, I glimpsed for the first time what it must be like to be an Aboriginal Australian, having to beg for acceptance in your own country, and then to be refused, to be shut out and despised, not for anything done, but for who you were.

Until these two incidents I'd thought of Australia as fundamentally decent, a society based on tolerance and equality of opportunity, the right of everyone to a 'fair go'. That belief had been shaken a little, it is true, by the events of November 1975 when the elected Federal Government was dismissed by the Governor-General. But I'd put that down to the machinations of power.

Now I began to be aware of a group of Australians for whom this idea wasn't true, the original inhabitants of the country who'd had their land taken from them by force and without compensation. Their kin had been killed, sometimes deliberately and systematically, sometimes more or less accidentally by us passing on our diseases. We'd robbed them of their traditional sources of food, condemning them to poverty. We'd tried to destroy their culture, so depriving their lives of purpose and dignity.

Earlier intuitions began to fall into place: the feeling I'd had at times coming home from school waiting for the bus and looking down the railway line running along what had once been a grassy valley between hills. I recall feeling somehow sad for the land which had been covered with asphalt roads, brick and concrete buildings, steel railway lines.

I remember an even stranger feeling on occasion in the bush when I sensed something there which did not like me, and the childishly romantic idea I occasionally had of an ancient, as yet undiscovered Empire somewhere in the centre of Australia (I'd obviously been reading Rider Haggard).

Now I began to understand that we non-Aboriginal Australians are intruders and that before we arrived the country was vastly different, mapped in different ways. Every rock, waterhole, valley, mountain and stream was part of an intricate system of knowledge, part of a culture that lived in tune with the land according to its rhythms.

This sounds rather romantic I suppose. But I'm someone inclined to look for a larger pattern of meaning than those provided by television, newspapers and advertisements. I also think that, as Marx put it, history weighs 'like an Alp' on the shoulders of the present. What has happened in the past continues to influence us in the present. It can be positive to the extent that we acknowledge, try to understand and learn. But it can be negative if we deny and repress.

This is all very theoretical. But I learned also that I'm

involved practically. Researching our family history, my sister discovered that our maternal great-great-grandfather, newly arrived from Ireland in the late 1830s, had taken up a block from a settler occupying land originally allocated as an Aboriginal reserve. So my family had taken part, however indirectly, in the dispossession of Aboriginal people.

This doesn't mean that our great-great-grandfather was particularly wicked – he was a poor man from Ireland in need of land. But it does mean that his good fortune, which became ours was built on Aboriginal misfortune, and that's something we should understand.

This is not to say we should go back to Europe. We are here to stay, and Europeans have brought many good things to this continent. The point is that we also need to take into account and respect the original culture, acknowledge our debt to its Aboriginal inhabitants who looked after the land so long, admit our offences against them and make what compensation is possible.

It is easy to idealise and fall victim to the Noble Savage syndrome, waxing lyrical about traditional Aboriginal culture and its harmony with nature. We can invent for ourselves an image, or, better, a fetish, of Australia as Arcadia and of Aboriginal people as simple children of nature. A fetish is an object believed to possess magical or spiritual power, and in the midst of the rush and complexity of their lives many people today find it comforting to cling to the magical thought of a people and culture somehow exempt from the pressures we feel. But this is only to reverse, not to banish, the world-view of imperialism in which 'black' is represented as evil and inferior. It is also to ignore the problems facing us in the present, retreating into an imaginary and highly idealised past.

True, this retreat is difficult in Western Australia. Events like the confrontation at Noonkanbah, the meeting in the Swan Valley and the strangely erratic reporting of the *West Australian* newspaper keep the real problems of violence and misunderstanding ever present. Ignoring the Australian Journalists' Association's code of ethics, in the past especially, the paper often identified people in conflict with the law as Aboriginal. On one occasion it featured on the front page a large photograph of an obviously Aboriginal youth who had been convicted in the Children's Court of a series of sex crimes.

On another occasion, significantly the day on which the companies of Alan Bond, who at that stage was the paper's main shareholder, had made a record loss, a day on which nearly every other newspaper in Australia made that their front page story, the *West Australian*'s headline was 'Aboriginal Gangs Terrorise Suburbs'. The story was about a small group of Aboriginal youths who had been robbing bottle shops and damaging property in one of the outer suburbs. The stereotype of Aboriginal people as enemies of decent society, drunken, lawless and lazy, had been further strengthened.

So it's not surprising that many West Australians have very strange ideas about Aboriginal people. Nor is it surprising that divisions between Aborigines and non-Aborigines run deep? Through Sister Peg Flynn, a friend and fellow member of my community, however, I began to make friends with Aboriginal people and to see how they were obliged to live. Her father had been a country doctor and she had always had a sense of obligation towards Aboriginal people. So when failing eyesight forced her to retire as principal of a primary school she chose to live in a little house in Gnowangerup, a prosperous town in the south-east with a sizeable Aboriginal population and a reputation for racism. (Disguised under the name of Norton, it served as an example of a prejudiced town in the 1975 Australian Government's Inquiry into Poverty.)

Her house became a drop-in centre for the Aboriginal children and later for their parents, the women especially. From time to time I would go to stay with her. There I began to see at first hand what it's like to be an Aboriginal person in a country town; the men with no work and no apparent future and nothing to do, apart from occasional forays into the bush hunting for kangaroos. Otherwise it was sit around and drink, with the older women trying to look after the men and the younger women and children,

And the children, lively, mischievous, active, hating school and loving sport, strangely innocent and affectionate. I also heard about the young men who ended up in gaol or were killed on the roads, the doctor who sometimes refused to admit Aboriginal people to the local hospital, and the girls who disappeared to Perth.

I saw a drunken white youth drive his utility directly at a group of Aboriginal children playing in the street, I also realised that most non-Aboriginal Australians did not want to know about all this or, if they did, did not care. They preferred to blame Aboriginal people themselves for the lives we've obliged them to live, having dispossessed them of their land, their language and much of their traditional culture.

So what does all this mean? I think it suggests that however we like to think of ourselves as living in a modern, even postmodern society, in Australia generally and in Western Australia in particular we still live on the frontier, at a point of encounter between cultures, between the known and the unknown, the past and the present.

A frontier is like a skin: it separates and holds together at the same time. Life is a matter of exchange, of dialogue and growth, not of static and unchanging totality, and this encounter is necessary for growth. Aboriginal Australia offers us another world view, one more sensitive to the environment and puts us in touch with a larger tradition of living and being than the opportunities presented by our culture.

It also offers us a different view of ourselves. As events at Noonkanbah and in the Swan Valley, the death of John Pat and the subsequent Royal Commission into Aboriginal Deaths in Custody, my experiences at Gnowangerup and the hysterical reactions to the Mabo decision suggest, we aren't as innocent as we like to think. Our overall treatment of Aboriginal Australians continues to be shameful.

To say this is not to make others feel bad, or to become part of the 'guilt industry'. On the contrary, if one accepts Paul Ricoeur's definition of guilt as feeling responsible for not being responsible, feeling somehow culpable yet refusing to acknowledge this culpability, then those who will not face the truth of history and refuse to come to terms with it are the ones trading in guilt. Those prepared to recognise the offences of the past and turn them into something different will forge a new relationship between the two peoples and cultures, one based on reconciliation rather than denial or confrontation.

This reconciliation has to be based first of all on historical memory, on the recognition of the wrongs of the past and the obligation which then follows to make some restitution. This recognition puts paid to the unimaginative, if not silly, argument that Aborigines today are given 'special privileges'. As the brief glimpses I've had of the lives of Aboriginal people in Western Australia today, even of those who've apparently 'made it', make clear, they are still profoundly disadvantaged, seldom treated as equals, are often despised, and must continually fight for recognition and respect. Unless Australian society is to be forever divided, repeating the past South African model, we need to base our reconciliation on communication, on mutual understanding and respect.

There could hardly be two more different cultures than the one we bought with us from nineteenth century Britain, almost entirely detached from the cosmic and religious dimensions of existence, and traditional Aboriginal culture with its profound sense of reverence and ritual. So far, we non-Aborigines have remained largely ignorant and contemptuous of that culture. Consequently we have also remained curiously rootless, without much sense of value apart from money and material possessions. True, we mostly are well-meaning, often generous and kind. Yet we are also strangely clumsy, almost illiterate, in matters of feeling and intuition.

Even those of us who call ourselves 'believers' seem to separate belief from our ordinary lives, lack a map of the spirit to guide our practical actions. As A G Stephens[*] observed in 1905, Australian society is thus profoundly secular. He wrote:

[*] A G Stephens was the Literary Editor of the *Bulletin* from 1895 to 1906.

There is in the developing Australian character a sceptical and utilitarian spirit that values the present hour and refuses to sacrifice the present for any visionary future lacking a rational guarantee.

It seems the religion we brought from overseas has not taken firm root in this land, and this may be the reason why we're unable to face the truth of our dealings with Aboriginal Australia: if there is no God, no merciful power beyond ourselves, then there is no forgiveness: to admit our fault imprisons us in the fault.

So we project the evil onto our victims, the Aboriginal people, making them responsible for what we've done to them, despising them as violent, lazy, irresponsible, drunken ...

This fear of who we are and what we've done, empowered and justified by the imperial fantasy that 'white' is to 'black' as good to evil, seems to me the cause of the invisible wall we've built between us and our Aboriginal brothers and sisters. This wall will tumble only when we learn to stand with them on the common ground of our humanity and learn with them that there are more things in heaven and earth than are dreamed of in a merely material world-view.

Essentially, then, the matter of our relations with Aboriginal Australians depends upon the answers we give to the three great philosophical questions: what do I believe in? What can I hope for? What must I do?

Traditional Aboriginal culture represents a way of being rooted in the past, in the living world and in the moral universe which we've lost in pursuit of material rewards. It is a culture which acknowledges the needs of the spirit as well as the body, seeing human beings as part of the larger web of existence, not as lonely individuals in competition with one another.

In it, to quote Simone Weil, 'this world and some world beyond, in their double beauty, interact, enriching and empowering each other'. Within this larger reality people have obligations to themselves, others and the world, obligations of respect expressed by the way we meet their physical and spiritual needs. So it is a world which is ethical through and through, ethics being a matter not just of private behaviour. It is also a matter of power and the sharing of power, of the ways in which we negotiate and accept a common way of life which enables us to live peacefully, happily and prosperously with others and the world.

For me the Aboriginal presence of which I was only dimly aware for so long, but which has been growing stronger and stronger over the last few years, speaks of this kind of possibility, one which is also central to my own beliefs as a Christian. If I'm right, then the question of relations between Aboriginal and non-Aboriginal Australians is a matter of our recovering our sense of a world beyond ourselves. It means shifting out of the narrow confines of merely utilitarian values and a world-view based on struggle and survival, and moving into a larger sense of reality. The walls between us are real but they are not necessarily permanent. As the Austrian poet Willy Verkauf Verlan writes:

> If the walls between us
> were made of glass
> we'd have shattered them
> long ago
> and we'd have walked
> over the pieces
> to each other.
>
> But the walls
> between us
> are invisible.
> They are hard to penetrate
> since they run through
> our hearts and spirits.

13

A LONG, LONG WAIT TIME

Bill Bunbury

As a boy, growing up in very green, rural Somerset, 16,000 kilometres from the land where my father had been born, I was strongly aware of an antipodean tug. My father spoke often about his own childhood in the bush between Nannup and Busselton. There were pictures to prove it, yellowing photos of doughty, fiercely moustached men in rolled-up shirtsleeves and collarless shirts, of pioneer homes like 'Cattle Chosen' where my father was born in the year of Australian Federation.

And there were small but vivid reminders of the original Australians, like the impressive kodj axe that hung on the wall of my father's study, an axe that I was later to bring back to Australia and present to the Western Australian Museum. There were tales too of clashes with the Noongar people; a pioneer, George Layman, had been speared. In the family's eyes I recall this made him a martyr. The Aboriginal people were part of the perils of the bush, like snakes, bushfire and flood. They were an invisible threat, part of the wilderness that my family had helped tame.

But my childhood was English, in one way subtly hued, where I lived, with legends of the Celtic past, Arthurian legend and older, more mysterious races, people who had raised the strange stone circles of Stonehenge and Avebury, of Harold the Saxon king, who had fallen at the Battle of Hastings, betrayed already by the perfidious Normans. A lot of my heroes were losers. But far less subtle was bristling Britishness; our primary school geography teacher, in 1947, pointing with pride to pieces of the world on which the British sun never set. And I suspect most of us thought of the world, if we thought at all, in terms of the red on the atlas. The indigenous people were part of the landscape, like the pages of our children's annuals. There were always the loyal natives, of course, helping the white men swim the flooded river and drive off hostile tribes.

Secondary school was Shakespeare and the Tudors and Stuarts. And university literature more of the same. At their very limits the boundaries were still European.

At the age of twenty-three I came to Australia fresh from English university life, impelled mostly by curiosity but also by a sense that this land had also always been part of my awareness. Australia was to prove another kind of university, but much more in the open learning mode. And it took a long time to absorb its most important lesson. Yet all the pointers were there.

I had only been in Western Australia three months when a elderly relative suggested we see something of the South-West. I was to drive his car and he would point out the sights. In the late afternoon of Day Two the blue bulk of the Stirling Ranges rose ahead on an almost empty road. I was about to meet Aboriginal Australians for the first time. A battered brown Holden stood stranded on the bitumen verge. A woman, clutching an old coat round her thin dress against the cold, waited with a child by the open bonnet, while her husband tried to restart a dead engine.

I pulled off onto the gravel. 'Don't waste your time,' I was told. 'They'll only ask you for money.' They didn't. I couldn't revive the dead engine but I promised I'd pass the word on at the next fuel station. I don't know to this day whether anyone came out for them. I got back into the car and drove on. There was little conversation for the next half hour. I felt that my attitude had only revealed to my elders how impetuous youth could be. I had learnt my first lesson about 1960s attitudes towards the original Australians.

Other lessons were to come much later and with far more force. Yet there were proddings. I recall a situation some years later at the boys' boarding-school at which I was then teaching. A dance had been planned with a nearby girls' school. A teacher from that college rang up the day before. Did the boys mind that one of the girls coming was an Aboriginal scholarship student? Would this cause any problems? No, the male teacher at our place assured her, but he would just check with the boys. Looking back, I don't know why she rang or why he felt any need to check. I can recall his dismay when the boys told him no one would be going if there was a 'boong' there. To his credit, he told them that they were right about that. That was in the mid-1960s.

At the same time and at the same school, there was an Aboriginal student, a natural athlete, if I remember rightly. He was difficult to reach, often silent in class discussion. I wish now that I had known how to come closer to his world. And given the student attitudes of his peers, and almost certainly their parents, I can see now what he probably endured, despite his popularity on the footy field.

By 1983 I had worked for the Australian Broadcasting Commission for fourteen years. In May that year my unit in Sydney sent me to Roebourne in Western Australia's North-West. I was to make a documentary about Aboriginal-police relations in that community. A young Aboriginal man, John Pat, had died in police custody. A trial was impending and the broadcast had to be made under sub judice conditions.

My time in Roebourne taught me many things. I learnt not only about police-Aboriginal relations but about relationships between the police and the white community. What I came to understand and appreciate most was Aboriginal endurance. This community had gone through extraordinary and destructive change, but was still trying to anticipate a better future. I sat and talked for a long time with Woodley King, a man who had overcome alcoholism and was now helping younger people find meaning in their lives. He took them out bush to give them experience of the country and bush skills.

People of Woodley's generation and older had not always

lived at Roebourne. Their original lands had lain further inland, lands also sought by the Pilbara pastoralists in the late nineteenth century and won at the expense of the original owners.

Aboriginal culture could and did survive this change, with some losses, as long as tribal families still lived on and worked the stations. The granting of equal wages in the 1960s and the subsequent shedding of cheap labour brought further dispossession and finally loss of country. Aboriginal tribes drifted into Roebourne, first to the reserve, and later to a new community, euphemistically called The Village.

Roebourne was part of the old North-West, a police depot and a base for pastoralism, a North-West that was soon to change with unbelievable swiftness. In the early 1970s the mining boom had taken off. New railways raced across the Pilbara. Mushroom towns, roads and airports appeared. And a new all white, almost entirely male workforce converged on the Pilbara. It was a good place to come for a job, unless you were Aboriginal. Despite the opportunities offered by mineral development and its associated activities, Aboriginal unemployment in the Pilbara remained high.

Single white men crowded into Roebourne's bursting pubs. Some Aboriginal women found uneasy employment as the only available females, and their male counterparts drifted into the isolated Aboriginal bars to drink away boredom and lack of meaning.

Those were the conditions under which John Pat met his death in 1983, a death which seemed at the time to symbolise the possible fate of the whole community.

And yet men like Woodley King and John Pat's own relatives could still foresee a future, and try to restore the self-respect and self-belief of the people around them. Those who have seen the remarkable film *Exile And The Kingdom*, presented by the late Roger Solomon and directed by Frank Rijavec, will know just how far they have reaffirmed their culture since 1983.

For me those weeks in Roebourne in 1983 were a final awakening point, a point when I had to say, 'How come I had never known this before?' I guess I had known before in my head, but not in the rest of my being. Roebourne was the physical reality, the result of several overlapping and tragic histories.

And there were no obvious targets. You could point to the police until you realised how poorly they were prepared for contact with Aboriginal communities. And if the police were racist, as many Aboriginal people alleged, what did that say about the community which those police represented?

Until I went to the Pilbara I had seen glimpses, but never the whole picture, of what must have happened to the tribes in the South-West where my family had farmed. It was at Roebourne that I realised what it would be like to lose your identity both as an individual and as a group. And it was also at Roebourne that I saw the seeds of success. The patient endurance of men like Woodley King may, in the end, prove stronger than the upheaval and the cultural destruction of the 1960s. I hope so, anyway.

And since Roebourne?

I have been at dinner parties and realised that bright chatter around tables still betrays both ignorance and assumption about the first Australians; chatter that expressed irritation at Aboriginal 'jabbering'. I found myself talking about people I'd met in the North-West who could speak eight tribal languages as well as English.

And once, researching a program about language, I went to visit an Aboriginal teacher at a school. We walked across the oval and continued our conversation inside the staff room. Another teacher was marking books and also our dialogue, which at that point was about Aboriginal identity. 'But you aren't a real Aborigine,' he told my friend. 'I mean, you dress like us and you read books.'

Since 1983 I have continued to interview, document and write about Aboriginal issues and Aboriginal-European history. Some still stand out. It was Dean Collard who told me how, as a boy in the country, his white playmate had asked him out to his parents' farm for the weekend, an invitation he shamefacedly retracted under family pressure. As Dean Collard recalled:

> *... they couldn't accept that an Aboriginal person was going to go out there. I mean that really made me feel low. I didn't ever get out there to see him or his farm.*

Aboriginal leader Rob Riley once told me that however committed Europeans might be to Aboriginal issues:

> *... they would never fully understand or appreciate because they have never had the experience of being an Aboriginal in Australia.*

I don't think that should stop us trying.

14

COLOURED LENSES AND SOCIAL RELATIONSHIPS

Catherine H Berndt

Because this is mainly a personal statement, I begin with two episodes which made a great impression on me at the time.

When I was about four, my mother, brother and sister and I went to live with our great-aunt in an inner suburb of Auckland. One day I was sitting at the back door on a low step facing across a concrete expanse towards a high wall of lattice and greenwork. Suddenly through it came what I saw as a frightening phenomenon taking up the whole of the gateway, in dark clothes from head to toe, carrying a plaited basket. I couldn't see the face properly, but it was the first time I had seen a tattooed chin, a moko.

When I cried out in fear, my mother came running. She didn't comfort me. Instead, she scolded me, telling me that this was a lady selling kumara, sweet potatoes, that I should be polite to a kind visitor and remember that other people had feelings too. She apologised to the visitor for my bad behaviour, and bought all the kumara.

However, I hadn't learned my lesson. I was a slow learner. When I was almost six, my mother took me to pre-primary school for the first time and I found that I was to be seated at a desk next to a tall, dark-skinned boy from Fiji. I cried and didn't want to sit next to him. So I was reprimanded for that, too. He was one of a large family. A year or so later his younger sister (lighter brown in skin colour) became one of my friends. She came to my birthday party, and I took her upstairs to introduce her to my great-aunt.

Words (including colour words), along with body language and signs and signals of various kinds, are crucial in human communication. During initial contacts and in unfamiliar situations, people seek clues that will help them gauge the attitudes and activities or actions of other people and help them frame their own responses. Deliberately or subconsciously, we register items which seem to be the same as things we're accustomed to seeing, or things that are quite strange. Of course, mistakes are possible in any kind of assessment of this sort. And the original intentions and plans may go ahead regardless of circumstances.

In any case, there is no way in which all the relevant information about the socio-cultural or personal contexts of such encounters, past and present, can be recorded or reported or observed or absorbed by any of the participants. Even the largest encyclopaedias or other means of storage and presentation of information are necessarily selective. Moreover, some people find them too daunting and long-winded, and look for easier modes of communication, easier access to meanings, simple stories, or personal conversations and opinions.

In Australia, until just recently, most of the general population, it seems, was not interested in Aboriginal culture – or even in the contact between Aboriginal people and others. The situation is changing in this respect. More material is becoming available. More people of Aboriginal descent are in a position now to tell their own stories, or write or illustrate their own experiences, without having to rely on the efforts of intermediaries.

With increasing population size, and partial or nominal intercultural mixing within Australia and beyond, comes the growth of information on a wider and larger scale. This has led to a growing demand for simplicity-within-complexity, a demand for easier access to such material and at the same time the continuation of convenience words.

These are words about which people say, 'We all know what that means', but which cover a wider range of double or multiple meanings: for example, 'white' and 'black', 'east' and 'west'.

Some years ago in New Zealand the written material available on Australian Aborigines was almost entirely negative. When I left my homeland early in 1940 to study Anthropology at Sydney University I met a student who had other views about Aborigines. He had been an honorary ethnologist at the South Australian Museum and had a number of Aboriginal friends.

In 1941, Ronald Berndt and I were married and started a lifetime of research and study, mainly in Aboriginal Australia, with other trips overseas including Papua New Guinea and a survey of Anthropology in India for the Indian University Grants Commission in 1965.

My introduction to field research and to Aboriginal Australia came at a place on the edge of the Great Victoria Desert. Ooldea was a small siding on the Trans-continental railway line. Some six kilometres behind the sandhills was a mission station by a small soak. We camped with our two small tents on the sandhills above the mission on the track which led to the Aboriginal camp, which was not static at that time.

Ron had been to Ooldea the previous year on an expedition with the Board for Anthropological Research and already knew some of the men. My main problem was that most of the women did not speak more than a few words of English and they didn't all speak the same dialect of the Western Desert language.

Ron had dark hair and skin that tanned very easily. In contrast I had fair hair and pinky-pale skin; but if that was a disadvantage or advantage as far as the women were concerned, they didn't have anything to say to me about it. It did not seem to matter to them, partly perhaps because I was young and eager to learn and they did not expect much of me. I was not an authority figure, and I was happy to have people who were ready to teach me. If they found me tiresome, they were too polite to show it. Usually they were very willing to help. When they were not and had other things to do, they didn't hesitate to let me know.

I used to go to the camp to talk, and listen, or some of the women would come to our camp and sit with me in the sandhills among the acacia bushes. I made mistakes, of course, in that preliminary period. For one thing, I wore denim overalls which were not, at that time, an acceptable form of dress for Aboriginal women. They did not think it was appropriate, but they forgave me for that, or seemed to forgive me. After all, for many of them, the place was as strange to them as it was to me. Many of the women had come from the central deserts and ranges in the spinifex country to the north.

From time to time during our six months at Ooldea little parties would come in, heading south towards the railway line, looking for flour, tea and sugar and other such commodities, and some mission helper would rush out and meet them, carrying clothes for adults and for children 'so they would not be obliged to come into the area without clothes on'.

Some newcomers, as well as people who had been in the area for much longer, were becoming accustomed to a kind of colour-mix and people-mix, in the small local population of fettlers and gangers and their families along the railway line, the small number of missionaries down at the soak, with their goats, and further along the line was a little tent at Wynbring Siding where Daisy Bates gave her handouts to any Aborigines who chose to visit.

I learned a lot from that period at Ooldea. And that was also true of the second period of research in the following year. Albert Karloan, one of the Yaraldi people from the lower River Murray and the Lakes, was focusing his life on brooding about the past. He was the last initiated man in his area to survive, and it worried him that he was unable to write his life story to pass to the other people of the area who did not know what the traditional culture had been like.

He asked Ron to undertake the task. In those days we had no electronic aids – no tape-recorders, not even ballpoint pens. We spent several months, on and off, with Albert and other people, trying to record everything he remembered. The last Aboriginal woman to be initiated in that area, Pinkie Mack, went on helping us after Albert Karloan's death.

We were not able to proceed then with publishing this material as Albert had wanted us to do. We had to go north. But that book is now complete: *A World That Was ...* (1993). We know that Albert would have been happy to see it, and so would Pinkie. The whole area of the lower River Murray and the Lakes was subjected to a great flood of colonisation in the nineteenth century, including a mission station whose missionary was interested in writing about Aboriginal culture but saw no place for it in real life. Most of the Aboriginal population spoke English and few knew much of their original traditional culture. The majority had quite pale skin and some had passed into the wider community.

When we came to Murray Bridge to be closer to Albert Karloan we camped among a group of people on an unofficial Aboriginal reserve, which meant that visitors from the outside world could come and go without needing permits. We were regarded as part of the Aboriginal community, many of whom were of lighter skin than we were. We did not need to change our colour to be regarded in that way.

One evening I was sitting on the ground outside our tent cooking dinner over an open fire. A couple of the visitors asked my husband how many wives he had. Was I the only one? They asked other personal questions too without any shame or reticence.

The official position in regard to Aborigines at that time, in that area and others, was that Aborigines should be absorbed into the larger community. It was a time of the assimilation policy, or at least, the preliminaries to that policy. Aboriginal life was hedged about with negative regulations, and Aboriginal people who had 'achieved citizenship' were not permitted to live on Aboriginal reserves or visit relatives who did.

We were criticised by officials for our 'encouragement', as they put it, of people of Aboriginal descent to maintain their traditional heritage, or at least to be proud of that heritage and not to lose sight of it. We were told, 'These are not real Aborigines, and it is no use pretending that they are'.

Our field of anthropology included, along with ordinary research, practical or applied aspects: welfare aspects, listening to people and what they wanted, and seeing how we could help them. For that reason, in 1944 we took a position arranged by Professor Elkin and Mr Chinnery (at that time Director of Native Affairs in the Northern Territory) as Welfare Officers and Anthropologists on Vestey's (Australian Investment Agency) Northern Territory stations. Our job was to look into practical aspects of Aboriginal welfare. It didn't work out as we'd hoped, for our reports made little impact on Vestey. Our final report on what we'd done, along with our study of conditions on the Aboriginal Army Settlements in the Territory, are detailed in the volume *End of an Era* (1987).

We had a difficult time on those stations. The Aboriginal people living there regarded us as their friends who would help them when needed and whenever we could.

To use just one example, an outstation on the Northern Territory side of a Western Australian station was one where we spent several months in a very difficult situation. It was a time of drought. Small parties of Aborigines who headed south into the Tanami desert came back puffy and exhausted, reporting that water was scarce and food even scarcer.

At one stage we tried to get food for the Aboriginal workers and their dependants on that outstation, to replace the stinking beef that had been allocated. The overseer was more than usually antagonistic to us. He nearly always went armed with a rifle and a pistol. One of his favourite pastimes was to shoot into the ground around several old blind Aboriginal men, laughing to see them jump. He tried to force us at gunpoint to go south to Tanami, shouting that we were not welcome about the place, and that we could go and starve down there. It was a rather awkward episode, not least because we could see several Aboriginal men, who knew what we were doing, dragging spears between their toes in the dust, waiting to attack him. That would have meant a police visit. In the end the temporary cook (who was ordinarily a wolfram miner) managed to persuade the overseer that it wasn't worth the trouble to get rid of us, and he thought the whole thing ought to be allowed to die down. There were other similar episodes.

Later on, in a very different setting, we supported the Methodist Mission in Arnhem Land in a protest against allowing tourists to set up villages on mission stations along the Arnhem Land coast. We were also in favour of keeping Arnhem Land as an Aboriginal reserve when the Northern Territory Administration wanted to throw it open (see our book *Arnhem Land: Its History and Its people*, 1954). Our views were not shared by numbers of people in the south, including some Aboriginal people. They claimed that such Reserves were a form of 'apartheid'.

Many people today, especially younger people, seem unaware of the part that the Methodist Overseas Mission played in this section of the Arnhem Land story – especially through the work of the Northern Territory chairman for some years, the Rev. Arthur Ellemore.

The Mission tried to work through the family unit (no dormitories), and encouraged people to use their own Aboriginal names and to speak their language. It chose to focus on one dialect of that language, and it tried to find a positive place in Christian teaching for what it saw as the best elements of Aboriginal religion. Despite massive mining ventures in the area in recent years, and other intrusive 'developments', Arnhem Land remained an official reserve and has done so virtually to the present day.

The people living there are convinced they have and still own their own territory, their own land and their own cultural heritage which has continued almost uninterrupted for a very long period indeed. Their heritage has had a formidable influence on the rest of Australia – Aboriginal and non-Aboriginal – in the areas of politics and land rights claims, art and song, particularly in the north-eastern side of the region.

Arnhem Land people are secure in the knowledge of their own identity. They do not need to look for their 'roots' as so many people in other parts of Australia have found themselves obliged to do. And in their case, looking for their roots, declaring their identity, has for all but a few of them not been marked by a change in skin colour as it has in so many other places.

A further personal point. My mother's family knew that her parents (and our great-aunt) were born in Nova Scotia; their parents came from the west of Scotland at the beginning of last century in a fleet of ships led by Norman McLeod. In the early 1850s they left Nova Scotia and travelled via Australia to the north of New Zealand.

My father's family was another matter. His mother (with a Scots name, but all we have of her is a photograph) died when he was born, and his father sent him away to someone who we believe was her mother in Australia. His father married again and fathered a tribe of children, but our father did not come back to New Zealand until he was a young man. After a short service in the First World War, he married my mother.

The marriage did not last long. He was sent back to Australia just before my brother was born. He came back when I was about twelve, hoping for a reconciliation with my mother. She agreed and went to live with him in Wellington. I stayed in Auckland with my great-aunt. After our mother died our father married again. We did not speak to him much about his background. We did not know, for instance, that his father was still living in 1935 in the Auckland area.

There was some talk in other branches of our father's family about a Maori connection, but the older people denied this. Our father's eldest brother told his grandchildren when they asked him about it, 'Our family starts with me', insisting there was no need for them to look further into the past.

But times were changing in New Zealand, and people were looking closely at the benefits as well as the disadvantages of having Maori ancestry. Some of our cousins were searching for more than the slender information they had inherited. One unexpected find was a pale man from Wiltshire, in England, only 150 centimetres high, who denied a charge that he'd stolen a horse and bridle. His death sentence was commuted to a trip to Sydney in 1819; he got his Ticket-of-Leave in 1828. His wife and three children followed him as free citizens, but both parents were dead by the early 1830s. One of their sons left Sydney for New Zealand. He was married late in 1839 to a Maori girl whose original home country had been in the Coromandel Peninsula until that area had been devastated in the Musket Wars by the Ngapuhi. Some people were left dead, and slaves were taken up to the Bay of Islands area.

So our great-great-granny was born in the north. She bore three sons to our English great-great-grandfather. The middle son was our great-grandfather. Her younger brother, Hori Pokai, has his photos and portraits in the well-known collection of portraits by Goldie at the Auckland War Memorial Museum. He did not die until about 1921, in Thames. Our great-great-granny's middle brother was named in one of the Auckland newspapers in the 1860s for threatening and actually trying to bring a Maori war canoe fleet into Auckland harbour in answer to a breach of tapu (sacredness) that had been suffered by his father. There are plenty of documents to demonstrate this connection, and more.

Our great-great-granny died quite young, in 1848/49, at Waiheke Island in the Hauraki Gulf, not far from the Coromandel Peninsula. Typically her husband (our great-great-grandfather), who died in a boating accident in the mid-1850s, had an inquest. A fair amount was written about the event, whereas her death went unrecorded in the official records.

My brother and sisters and I were happy to learn of this Maori connection, and to go through all the documents and newspapers, including the reference to the original canoe associated with our ancestors on that side.

We were interested in our other roots as well. The Scots side; the English side, with the little fellow and his wife from Wiltshire; and the Irish connections that I have not mentioned. We did not want to disown any of these roots. We saw them as a mosaic which has helped to make us who we are and that we delight in discovering. With the Maori connection we felt that we were joining the great number of Pakeha New Zealanders who were pleased to be personally connected with the land and its original inhabitants. It gave us a kind of toe-hold, a greater link with the ground on which we were born. Even though one part of our ancestry on that side was made up of the invaders, the non-Maoris, the Pakeha, whose genes we also carry within us, can we legitimately call ourselves 'brown people'?

Certainly we do not want to be called 'white people', for various reasons; not simply that we are not 'white' in colour, but of some other colour – pale or pinky or some-such, but definitely not 'white'.

In all human cultures, colour is also intrinsically an important ingredient, in a wide variety and in numerous dimensions, economic, political, symbolic, aesthetic. In Aboriginal Australia alone, black and white colouring is used for varying purposes: black, for example, as charcoal for skin decoration; white for skin decorations and painting, on bark and on the ground, on various objects. But white, mixed with ashes, could be used for mortuary purposes, for widows for instance, or smeared over the total body in hunting to cover the smell of sweat which might discourage the hunted animals; and red, of course, the colour of blood, symbolising blood, with red ochre as an especially important colour.

In western Arnhem Land, specific terms distinguish between pale and dark people, but there isn't the same stigma attached as there is in many areas these days to 'white' versus 'black'. There, as in some other areas, the term for 'white' can also indicate the idea of 'shining' or 'bright'. The term for darkness can signify either the black of night, or black of other substances.

In more general terms today, the words 'white' and 'black' are used more loosely to distinguish certain populations from others. These political slogans are, in a way, double-think or convenience words, which actually subsume under each heading a diversity of political alliances or attitudes and personal identities. A pale skin can be identified by its owner as 'black' and vice versa; or a 'black' person so-called can be said to have a 'white' heart. Some people talk about 'coconuts', 'brown' outside, 'white' inside, meaning that these people are in a way traitors to some political cause or attitude.

In the north of Australia, for a long time, Aborigines were

called 'blacks'. They were identified by the people who saw them as being of a black colour, which was really a matter of shades of brown. No wonder Aborigines turned the word 'black' to have a positive meaning which it did not enjoy in the days of the last century and sometimes does not have even now.

In their practical connotations, the words 'black' and 'white' are divisive, inflammatory and not conducive to harmony in social relationships. This is not asking that people should be colour-blind. On the contrary, some of the loveliest poems and songs in all cultures deal with such attributes as hair and eye colour in the aesthetic sense. It is the political implications and divisiveness of the terms used now that are alarming when it comes to interpersonal and political relations.

Skin colour, then, can be read as a badge suggesting or proclaiming social or political identity. Aesthetically, it can be seen as a matter of personal or cultural preference. More important is the recognition that it is superficial, 'only skin deep' or, to cite a saying in a different context, 'the Colonel's lady and Judy O'Grady are sisters under the skin'. In human relationships, between people *as* people, skin colour is, or should be, totally irrelevant.

15

THINKING IN COLOUR

Myrna Tonkinson

'Jurra! jurra! Walybala nyaangga' (Stop, stop there's a whitefella here). It took me a few seconds to realise that the person being referred to as 'whitefella' was me, a black woman. This was the first time I was aware of being so designated and it was something of a shock. It was 1974 during a ten month stay at Jigalong, a remote Aboriginal settlement in Western Australia, home of about 350 Mardu. An angry man was threatening to throw a boomerang, and was being cautioned that he might hit a 'whitefella', the prospect of which was expected to act as a deterrent.

This incident and a few other, less dramatic situations in which my status was discussed led me to reflect on my own identity as well as on the way that Aboriginal people classify themselves and others. It made me ponder also the fact that, notwithstanding anthropological knowledge, references to skin colour, and popular assumptions and expectations that link biology and culture, pervade our language and personal and social relationships. My experience among the Mardu exposed me to an alternative way of thinking about colour and identity.

As a woman of Afro-Caribbean ancestry, being labelled 'whitefella' was entirely alien to me. I grew up in Jamaica, a country with an ethnically mixed, but predominantly black, population. In Jamaica, minute gradations of skin colour are noted and named; even within my own family three or more colour terms would apply. There is no sharp dichotomous division of the population; there is an ideology of unity. Diversity is celebrated;

the country's coat of arms bears the motto: 'Out of Many, One People', though the reality is not identical with the ideal. The experience of slavery and the British colonial heritage left us with a tendency to accord higher status and, often, better employment and other opportunities to persons who were 'white' or of light skin colour. To a considerable extent, social class correlated with skin colour. This, not to mention the international dominance of Hollywood movies and other images that promote narrow Western ideals of beauty and worth, meant that I had firsthand knowledge of colour distinction.

Nevertheless, I grew up as part of a black majority. Most of our teachers, politicians, and other influential and powerful people were of similar background to my own. Being a black woman was a crucial component of my personal identity.

When I was twenty, in 1964, I left Jamaica for the first time and moved to Chicago as an immigrant. I discovered that in my new country, being black could have serious, even lethal, consequences. Unlike Jamaica, the tendency in the United States of America is to ignore gradations of colour. There, I discovered, any known African ancestry is somewhat like a taint that results in the carrier being labelled black and liable to suffer discrimination.

Racial discrimination was no longer legal in 1964, but, in effect, colour was and continues to be a factor affecting socioeconomic status. Neighbourhoods were distinctive not only along class lines but also in terms of ethnicity and colour, and I felt vulnerable if I found myself in the wrong part of town. In Chicago, I became part of a disadvantaged minority. Race as a concept with deep symbolic and real significance became part of my daily experience in new and disturbing ways.

Then, in 1973, I came to Australia where being black took on still other meanings. For the first time I was neither part of the majority nor of a distinct and stigmatised minority, but a single individual, exotic and sometimes an object of curiosity and even fear. I came with my Australian husband to the Australian National University and we lived in Canberra for three months before heading for Jigalong to do anthropological fieldwork. In

Canberra, even with its diplomatic missions and international university population, black people were a rarity.

In this country, I quickly discovered, skin colour and ethnicity were significant in ways that differed from, as well as paralleled, those evident in the United States of America. In the hierarchy of value, based on colour and culture, Aboriginal people were ranked firmly at the bottom. The first Aboriginal person I met was Harry Penrith (now Burnum Burnum), who was then a public servant, but is now best known as an author and cultural educator. He came and sat next to me on a bus on which we were the only two black people; a situation that was so rare that it resulted in instant presumption of comradeship.

In Sydney, where I had spent my first few days in Australia, the absence of Aboriginal people on the streets had been notable. Canberra seemed the same. Despite this, Aboriginal issues were very much in the news. The Aboriginal Tent Embassy had gone but there was feverish activity in Aboriginal affairs. There appeared to be genuine efforts to improve the conditions and advance the rights of Aboriginal people, among many other reforms being carried out by a Labor party so long denied power.

I find it interesting that now, twenty years later, Whitlam's time and his efforts to bring about change in Aboriginal affairs are forgotten or demeaned. Prime Minister Paul Keating has recently been described by several Aboriginal and non-Aboriginal people as the first Prime Minister to commit himself to real change for the indigenous population. While he is to be commended for his historic Redfern speech,* he is certainly not the first to take a public stand of this kind. The Keating government's legislative response to the historic High Court ruling on native title (the Mabo decision) is momentous and laudable. We should acknowledge, however, that changes introduced by past federal governments, particularly under Prime Ministers Whitlam

---

* In late 1992 Prime Minister Paul Keating launched the International Year for the World's Indigenous People. In his speech Mr Keating said the starting point in building a harmonious multi-cultural society for the future had to begin with recognition of the facts of dispossession.

and Fraser, helped pave the way for it.

Some of my own work in Aboriginal affairs took place in the area of land rights in the Northern Territory. The enabling legislation (the Aboriginal Land Rights [Northern Territory] Act 1976) is not flawless; it entails slow and costly processes and fails to address the needs of Aboriginal people whose dispossession was so complete that they could not prove traditional ownership of any vacant crown land. Nevertheless, it was a pioneering step that has not so far been equalled. I am happy to have had some involvement in the implementation of a process by which some Aboriginal people have regained some of their land.

In the late 1970s and early 1980s, working at the Australian Institute of Aboriginal Studies, as it was then known, I assisted the Central and Northern Land Councils of the Northern Territory to recruit anthropologists to prepare land claims. With a male colleague, I did the anthropological work for the Cobourg Peninsula claim which was settled through negotiation with the Northern Territory Government. I prepared a women's submission for the Nicholson River claim, in which most of the claimants lived on the Queensland side of the Gulf country. Later, I was the research officer for two Northern Territory Aboriginal Land Commissioners.

This work brought me into contact with many Aboriginal people, and afforded me opportunities to appreciate at first hand something of the richness and diversity of their cultures, as well as the parallels and continuities across vast areas. Working on land claims also enabled me to see some awesomely beautiful and remote places on this continent, in the Northern Territory, Queensland and Western Australia.

Aboriginal people with whom I had contact during the preparation and hearing of land claims were invariably welcoming, though often reserved. Sometimes they expressed curiosity about my background, and, occasionally, explicitly remarked on our similarity as black people. Yet, there was never any doubt that I was a stranger with a different cultural heritage. Several people at a Queensland settlement described me to my colleague as 'that dark lady where she come from overseas.'

When I went with my husband to Jigalong in February 1974, it was not his first trip there. He had begun fieldwork at the settlement in 1963 and had been back several times since, so he was returning to familiar people and places, to a language which he spoke well and a culture he had been studying for more than ten years. For me it was all new except for what I had read or been told. I experienced a mixture of emotions, including excitement, shock and apprehension after finally getting there. It is impossible to know how I would have been received had I arrived on my own or with someone who had not already established a close relationship with that community.

The Mardu welcomed me and quickly fitted me into their social structure. As the wife of someone who had already established fictive kin relations, and been given section ('skin') membership, my place was virtually a foregone conclusion. Both Bob and I expected that the Mardu might express some curiosity about me, the first non-Aboriginal black person to live among them. To our surprise, however, there was virtually no comment. In the few discussions I had with people about this I was never able to persuade them that my skin colour signified any special link with them, although on other grounds, I developed many close relationships. One elderly man was visibly moved after my account of how my ancestors had been taken from Africa as slaves, forced to relinquish their language and traditions and to work under brutal conditions. He concluded that I had suffered a great loss and should be taught as much as possible about his people's culture as a kind of compensation. However, I had no inkling of any sense of shared oppression on his part.

By Australian and international standards, people at Jigalong were living in conditions of appalling squalor and poverty. Despite what I already knew about the place, I was shocked to see it. No one was starving, or even inadequately nourished most of the time. However, many were dressed in shabby clothes; their homes were mostly self-built humpies of corrugated iron, bushes, canvas and whatever materials were available. Some people had even more uncomfortable and ugly one-room unlined metal boxes with a single window and a door, which passed for a house; cold in winter and unbearably hot in summer. Water was available only at a few strategic points around the settlement and there was no electricity. (While still far from ideal, this situation is now much improved.)

The contrast with conditions in urban Australia was stark, and, although by no means luxurious, the amenities enjoyed by the white people living at Jigalong were vastly superior. Most of the staff lived in old asbestos houses constructed during the mission days; others, like the teachers, had newer demountable houses. Our home was a four metre caravan, parked near the school and coupled to the teachers' house for electricity. I was acutely aware of how favourably my living conditions contrasted with those of the people in whose home community I was living.

Apart from such obvious differences in material conditions, being a 'whitefella' has other meanings. For the Jigalong Mardu, it implies a lack of cultural knowledge which renders most persons in that category unequipped to deal appropriately with certain situations. Being whitefella in Jigalong meant being protected, because of assumed ignorance, from the consequences of some actions and from many kinship obligations. It also excluded most outsiders from participation in the supremely important ritual life of the community. Those in the whitefella category were often assumed to have limitless access to resources and expected to be available at anytime to provide certain services such as medical assistance or dealing with the dead.

I have written elsewhere that for many Aboriginal people, certainly those at Jigalong, colour is not the significant marker of culture, identity and worth that it is for white Australians. Some scholars dispute this, but, as I see it, the tendency of people at Jigalong to place me in the category 'whitefella' is consistent with their giving salience to culture in determining status. Of course, this did not mean there was no recognition of phenotypic difference. I remember a teenage boy, visiting from another community, approaching me and asking tentatively: 'Mardun?' (Are you

Mardu/Aboriginal?) I also heard Japanese visitors referred to as mada mada, a colour term used for people of mixed Aboriginal-European descent.

Occasionally, people would enquire what my 'country' (meaning the land, rather than the political entity to which I belonged) was like, whether it was as 'lovely' or 'good' as theirs. I was sometimes asked if I came from the same country as Charley Pride (a black American country and western singer, who was very popular at the time), and if I knew him. African American actors in films also evoked similar comment.

It was obviously not skin colour but perceived culture, based on speech and interaction styles, among other things, that the Mardu were marking when they called me a 'whitefella'. I think they were also making an accurate assessment that I shared the different, and privileged, status enjoyed by whites. (I have also heard Jigalong people apply the whitefella label to people of mixed Aboriginal and European descent who enter the Jigalong community in their role as bureaucrats, and whose biographical details are unknown to the Mardu, and whose behaviour they perceive as 'whitefella' ways.)

The status implications of belonging to the whitefella category are clear enough to the Mardu even if they do not know the details regarding Australia's socio-economic indicators and other factors. Still, for the Mardu, the whitefella category is not homogeneous; they make finer distinctions when they deem it necessary. For example, Bob Tonkinson has reported that, when Jigalong was a mission, the Mardu (at Jigalong the label 'blackfella' is not used) distinguished between 'whitefellas' and 'Christians' to indicate the presence or absence of certain behaviours such as smoking and drinking.

In my experience, there is a marked tendency among Aboriginal people to take note of individual differences among people rather than assuming homogeneity among members of any particular category. I have seldom encountered an Aboriginal equivalent of the white Australian tendency to invoke stereotypes, often derogatory but sometimes patronisingly precious, when referring to Aboriginal people. A clear exception to this is the polemical statements of Aboriginal political leaders, who adopt the kind of rhetoric that is commonly found in white Australian discourse about 'race'.

In the politics of Aboriginal resistance and protest, the language of race, based on discredited but still popular assumptions about links between genetic inheritance and culture, is heavily used. This essentialist view of identity inevitably leads to biological determinist arguments and to stereotyping, and I find it perplexing and ironic that people who have been victims of such thinking can embrace it themselves.

In contrast, Jigalong people, and others with whom I have worked closely, rarely generalise from their negative experiences to condemn all white people, but seem to judge each person's behaviour on its own merits. Moreover, it is not uncommon to hear Aboriginal people express compassion for some of their former abusers. This tendency is not based on any stated ideal of charity or forgiveness, but on the powerful influence of familiarity in personal relationships. It indicates the multi-dimensional nature of such relationships, which of course is not unique to Aboriginal people, but which in their society seems to allow for great appreciation of individual differences and tolerance of contradictions in the behaviour of individuals. I have not seen much evidence that this tolerance is reciprocated.

Whether or not it was part of the perception of Jigalong people, my structural location in Australian society is decidedly closer to the whitefella end of the status spectrum than to theirs. Being whitefella, even for a newly arrived immigrant, means access to services and opportunities that are often unavailable to Aboriginal people. I am acutely conscious of the fact that, despite the realities of racism for all non-white people in Australia, many of us are shielded from its worst effects. Most immigrants, at least potentially, enjoy benefits of which most indigenous people have been deprived, legally in the past, and now as a de facto consequence of a history of exclusion and discrimination. Although many immigrants have suffered discrimination because of their language, culture or colour, the indignities endured by Aborigines are grotesquely unique. The newest migrant, especially if white, at least potentially has access to the privileges of white society including the liberty to join the chorus of instant experts who freely vilify the indigenous people of this country.

Someone like me confounds some whites because they see a highly educated middle-class black woman as a contradiction in terms. In this respect, my experience in Australia has differed from my Jamaican and American experiences. In Alice Springs I was deeply shocked to be called an 'armchair nigger' by an educator working with Aborigines. He seemed to be suggesting that I was not an authentic black person because I did not fit some familiar stereotype. Perth is the only place in the world where I have been attacked directly, in person and through the mail, by persons I did not know, simply on the grounds of my skin colour. However, I've never been refused access anywhere or suffered the contempt and denial of dignity that are the everyday experience of so many of Australia's indigenous people. My education and experience have enabed me to pursue a fairly protected middle-class life. Also, I have been well aware of my rights as a citizen of this country.

I have been amazed and embarrassed to see that black people like me have an exotic appeal in areas where indigenous Australians are rarely included. There has been a shift in recent years from depicting images of Australians as all-white and Anglo or Celtic, to showing a more accurate multi-racial and multi-cultural picture. However, Aborigines and Torres Strait Islanders are almost totally absent from this. We're far more likely to see an African American basketballer than an Aboriginal footballer used in promotions and advertisements.

Sometimes white Australians have sought to bestow upon me a kind of inclusion I do not seek or accept: of being one of the 'us' who are superior to 'them'. Some people have been surprised when, in response to this, I have shown anger and accused them of racism. Even many people who consider themselves enlightened and tolerant can engage in maligning Aborigines. It is as though the presence of the indigenous people were a reproach to many other Australians, engendering guilt and fear. If the indigenes cannot be ignored, then they must be characterised as unworthy in order to justify their condition, or even as being too well off, enjoying unearned benefits that are unavailable to whites. Some reactions to the Mabo decision sharply illustrate these prejudices.

At another extreme are those who represent Aboriginal people as innocent paragons, in harmony with nature, totally spiritual, free of materialistic values or aspirations, victims, not actors or agents. This no doubt well-meaning attitude denies Aboriginal people their humanity, resilience and adaptability. These views sometimes come from people who are disillusioned with their own culture and are seeking its foil among indigenous (read 'primitive') peoples.

Idealism of this kind often leads also to disillusionment when its objects are perceived as failing to live up to expectations. Romanticised images are often based on ignorance and are another way of designating people as 'other', obscuring shared humanity.

The policy of multi-culturalism has done much to ameliorate the negative consequences of being different in Australia, and has certainly resulted in changes in the Australian ethos. Multiculturalism has not meant the disappearance of racism, intolerance, stereotyping and other problems that beset non-Anglo-Australians. However, governments have set the tone for a broader definition of what being Australian means, and positive results are evident. The discourse that highlights Australia's links with its Asian neighbours also is having real, if gradual, effects on Australian identity. In much of this discourse, however, the indigenous population is strangely absent or, at best, marginal.

Cultural identity is denoted by three major categories in Australian popular discourse: 'Australians', who are white and of British or Irish heritage, or indistinguishable from those; 'migrants' or 'ethnics', who are from non-English-speaking and/or non-white backgrounds; and Aboriginal and Torres Strait Islander people who are the quintessential 'others' in Australia. Whatever the official policy, in practice multi-culturalism seldom embraces the indigenous Australians. This is a complex problem, since not only are the indigenes are excluded but they usually reject attempts to be incorporated as just another ethnic (meaning migrant, and not really Australian) group in multi-cultural Australia. As an Aranda man put it to me in Alice Springs in 1978: 'We not new Australian, we Aboriginal people.' This response is based on the accurate perception that the dominant Australian majority has appropriated to itself the status of authentic Australians and the prerogative of defining everyone else as 'other', using a variety of labels. Not surprisingly, most Aboriginal people want their unique status as indigenous inhabitants of this continent acknowledged.

Given their observation of the common pattern of foreigners entering Australia and gaining acceptance in the dominant culture, it is little wonder that some activist Aboriginal people show hostility to me as a privileged outsider, and an anthropologist to boot. They argue that like white outsiders, I have no business claiming any expertise on matters Aboriginal.

Although I have some sympathy for this view, I do not accept it. This is not simply because it is personally painful, but because I reject essentialist views of cultural identity. To me, the insider's view and the informed outsider's view of a culture both have validity. They can be complementary. They certainly need not be opposed or mutually exclusive. Social science is a valid endeavour, and its practice would be meaningless if only insiders were capable of gaining knowledge and understanding of societies and cultures. Moreover, such expertise does not follow automatically from membership of a group any more than expertise as an anatomist follows from having a body.

I do not deny that anthropology emerged as a discipline in Europe with colonised peoples as its main focus. Nor do I wish to justify objectification of the 'other' as a topic of research. Rather, it is my view that all humans are cultural beings; that cultural diversity overlays a basic shared humanity; that cultures can be studied; that being part of a culture may make one an expert practitioner but not necessarily an expert analyst of it; and that trained but empathetic observation and analysis can produce valuable cultural insights. Of course, the role of the expert is distinct from that of the representative; but one can speak about an issue without presuming to speak for the people concerned.

Sharing expert knowledge that enhances human understanding is desirable, both within academic circles and with the wider public. Such knowledge is vital in cases such as the current Mabo debate, in which outrageous, uninformed pronouncements have featured prominently. It is obvious, however, that many of those mounting the attack on the granting of native title are not interested in accuracy and are, indeed, wilfully ignorant.

Notwithstanding many differences, some of which I have outlined above, I share with Aboriginal Australians the status of the colonised and the experience of being black in a country (and indeed a world) dominated by assumptions of white superiority. Contradiction and paradox abound in relationships between blacks and whites, as in all complex situations. It seems, though, that most white Australians cannot be neutral or detached about us. Some invoke stereotypes, usually negative. Some see black people as representing otherness in archetypal, impersonal ways. We are often deemed exotic, and the exotic both attracts and repels. In many situations, being black means being ignored or treated with thinly veiled contempt, or being patronised. A friend told me of being asked by someone at her workplace where she came from. When she replied that she was Aboriginal, the enquirer responded sweetly, 'Never mind, dear.'

In such conditions it is difficult for black people, especially in minority groups, to develop and maintain positive self-image, strong cultural identity, and self esteem. I do not presume any intimate knowledge of the lived experience of being an indigenous Australian. Still, I have had intimations of it. For example, when I spent time in Alice Springs in the late 1970s, I experienced frequently an immediate stiffening and glowering on the part of many staff in shops and businesses as soon as I would enter. (A white colleague who visited me there remarked on this.) It was clear that this was a common reaction to Aboriginal people.

From the earliest British settlement right up to the present, Aboriginal Australians have been denigrated for not being like whites; for not having invented the wheel; for not practising agriculture; for not living in villages or towns; for not having writing. In the mind of many people, these are perceived as defects, inextricably connected with being black, and justifying the doctrine of terra nullius, the belief that even though they were here first, the indigenous people were not using the land in ways that would entitle them to any claim of prior ownership. In addition, whites having the upper hand set the terms by which the worth of persons in this country would be judged. Aboriginal and Islander people have been defined negatively, have been subject to deliberate programs to erase their cultural and, at times, even their physical characteristics, and have generally had their identity challenged.

Besides dispossession, dislocation, and the undermining of their cultural identity, the indigenous population has endured a number of devastating events and policies as a consequence of colonisation. They provided reliable, cheap labour for the pastoral industry for many decades and then were discarded when wage equity was required by law. Large numbers of their children were taken away to institutions. Being Aboriginal has also meant a high probability of being worse off than all other Australians according to all social indicators – for example, having a far shorter life expectancy than other Australians, being less healthy, less well educated, living in poorer housing, having a greater chance of being unemployed, and if employed earning lower incomes. All this is well known in statistical terms, and engenders shock and dismay in many of us. When one is confronted directly with the reality of these statistics of disadvantage, it is immensely distressing.

Among the Aboriginal people I know best, at Jigalong and related communities, these statistics have a poignant reality. In this population of fewer than 1,000 people, death is a frequent occurrence. Funeral ceremonies constitute the most common reason for inter-community travel. An alarmingly high proportion of deaths are among people aged between twenty and forty. Alcohol is implicated in many of these deaths even when it is not a direct cause. Accidents, illness and violence contribute to the awful toll.

Education is another area in which sharp discrepancies are evident between the Aboriginal and non-Aboriginal sectors of the Australian population. While there have been some impressive improvements in the education statistics in recent years, change has occurred unevenly and seems non-existent in some places. Thus, while there has been a remarkable increase in the number of Aboriginal people pursuing tertiary education in Western Australia, Jigalong children seldom attend high school. Post-primary education is available at the local school, but very few children go from there to high school. Skilled jobs in Jigalong are filled by outsiders, although there are local Aboriginal people employed as education workers, aides in the clinic, labourers on building projects and in other support roles.

Although Aboriginal cultural factors contribute to this state of affairs, I believe it is largely the result of a perception of Aboriginal people as outside mainstream Australia, inevitably and permanently. Despite the fact that English is a second language for children at Jigalong, and that the conditions to promote literacy are absent from their homes, they, and children like them in other Western Australian communities, are not seen by the Ministry of Education as requiring specialist teachers.

The teachers they get are often dedicated and conscientious; the schools have materials that acknowledge their culture. However, the methods and materials being used are not conducive to the achievement of outcomes expected for Australian children generally. After many decades of ignoring the needs of children from non-English-speaking backgrounds and forcing them to sink or swim in the normal English classrooms, there are now trained ESL (English as a Second Language) teachers and special programs for such children. The equivalent for

Aboriginal children, except in so far as they attend schools classified as disadvantaged which qualify for additional resources such as lunch programs has yet to be achieved.

In these circumstances, it is difficult not to feel frustration and despair. Yet I've been deeply impressed by the vitality and resilience of Aboriginal people, and there are some hopeful prospects. If governments do not thwart the process, Jigalong people stand a good chance of recovering native title to their traditional land in the Western Desert. This would be an immensely significant victory, but, by itself, will not necessarily improve the socio-economic status and general well-being of the Mardu. There is ample evidence of this danger from many Aboriginal communities in other parts of the country. Achievement of the national goal of reconciliation is, in my view, crucial. Genuine reconciliation must entail closing the wide gap between indigenous Australians and whitefellas in health, education, employment and all socio-economic indicators.

Reconciliation must include material forms of compensation. Essential too is acceptance of Aboriginal Australians as part of the diverse array of peoples and cultures that constitute this nation, while recognising their unique status as prior owners of this continent. To me, these are necessary steps to achieving a just society in which skin colour, while relevant to personal identity, will not determine one's social status – a society where being whitefella will no longer signify privilege when compared with indigenous Australians.

16

BEING WHITE WOMAN

Judith Wright

I am a fifth generation white Australian, which used to be a considerable boast when I was born in 1915. It might almost make me an indigenous person. But when I compare it to the real children of this country, it dwindles to nothing. I am one of the usurpers, not one of those who owned the land now violently stolen from them.

Aboriginal people say they have been here 'forever'. That is a claim we have never yet disproved – give or take a million years or so. Theories abound as to when and how they happened to be in Australia, and when or how that happened is still veiled in myths of origin; the ancestors left their stories but didn't feel it necessary to add dates and eras.

Aboriginal people also say, with complete truth, that they have never bargained with us, never admitted any right in us to take their land, never sold or exchanged or otherwise paltered with their own relationship with it – while we are always buying or selling, profiting from, and destroying, that land. We hardly dare to think what the financial compensation might be for those two centuries of usurpation and the resultant damage if we were ever to contemplate a decent deal with them.

The judgment of the high court in the Murray Islands' case (the Mabo judgment as the law knows it, though many of the other Islanders took part in it as well as Eddie Mabo) is therefore something that we have to accommodate in ourselves, as well as in our legal, educational, economic and historical systems. It is a challenge of immense implications for our European arrogance.

I might count myself lucky that the males of my family have been the landholders, and that the idea of women owning land is rather unfamiliar to white male Australians. It was almost at the end of a normal working life that I was able to buy (or to get a mortgage over) a patch of freehold land, something a little more than 40 hectares, cheap enough because of its stony and steep nature and its lack of pasture and timber. That achievement is rare for women, and it had its ironic side, since I don't believe in owning land. I feel a little as Aboriginal people do in that; land is sacred and a trust rather than a possession. The only way to claim land as an owner under the English-inherited land laws is to buy it – under what we call freehold; or to lease it for a term of years. The land one claims in either way was Aboriginal land, ranged over for uncountable years by those who lived their relationship with it, changing it by fire if it was becoming too overgrown for marsupials, otherwise harvesting its natural products for their use, which was light and undemanding. In that way, they survived great changes in climate and conditions over those many centuries – and thereby have incurred bitter accusations from us that they failed to use it in ways we believe necessary.

I love the country where I was born and brought up, even though by the time I arrived many changes had overtaken the land. Its original aspect had long been lost, as mobs of sheep and cattle took the place of kangaroos and wallabies, and new grasses and crops, roads and fences, altered it under the land laws and customs introduced by three or four generations of white people. The removal of the original owners had been so thorough that they seemed scarcely to exist in the world I lived in, except as a few stockmen and women sometimes employed in kitchen or laundry work, and a few silent people in the streets of Armidale, whom few people looked at, or recognised. Certainly not as the owners of the land.

Yet, as I later discovered from an old manuscript preserved in the New England University Library, it was not much more than fifty years before I was born that Wallamumbi, the station I had lived on, was in Aboriginal possession and that white men had been in terror of their resistance. The author of the manuscript had been employed as a shepherd and stockman there at a time when one had to carry a gun to do the work. The surviving building from those times was very solidly built of slabs, with heavy drop-shutters on the few window spaces. (Much of the original timber had already been cut when I was a child; those slabs must have come from the largest trees there at that time.)

That building was used as a store and harness-repair 'shop' (all the outbuildings were known as 'shops', from the 'blacksmith's shop' to the 'butcher's shop'). Now that harness and blacksmith work is no longer part of the life of most stations, perhaps that original building has been dismantled to make garages or other sheds with other purposes. History hasn't much time for the outmoded.

My father, who had a fairly good relationship with his staff and sometimes employed Aboriginal people on stock work or odd jobs, (paying them as his own parents had done), showed me an old and twisted tree with strange carvings on its trunk and said it was a 'sacred funeral tree'. It stood close to the shearing shed and is no longer there; I don't know its fate. He also had something of a collection of stone axes, and a 'bullroarer' on a string, which he could whirl to make a terrifying noise. I don't know how he came into possession of these or where they are now.

I found on the land I bought far to the south of Wallamumbi, many years later, a couple of chipped stones, scrapers or axes; most people put such things, if they were thought of any interest, into local museums as being the possessions of the finders (on the fine old maxim of 'finders keepers, losers weepers'). That was more or less, come to think of it, the way the country was taken. Along with that other maxim 'Might is Right', whole empires justify their existence in such ways.

I had gone so deep into the story of our times, in my research for *The Cry For The Dead*, and it was so horrifying, that for me the only way ahead lay in working for Aboriginal rights – not just for land, but for all those rights we had been, and were, denying them. Helping to get the Aboriginal Treaty Committee under way and working for it over the years from 1978 to 1983, when the Hawke Government made its lavish promises and our support naturally dropped away, was the way I chose.

Then came the betrayal of all those promises, and a massive attack by the industries opposed to any form of recompense for Aboriginal people and Torres Strait Islanders. Hawke's crocodile-tears as he left office were a fitting symbol of those years. If any government again tries to avert the fate of South Africa, the same thing will happen, and is indeed happening.

Before and after the publication of the book that summed up our efforts from 1978 to 1983 as a committee, I went on learning, and all I learned pointed in the same direction. Not only had we taken the land at gunpoint and introduced all the Western diseases and errors, we had attempted to break the spirits and culture of those incredibly ancient communities and tribes in all ways open to us. There was an arrogance about us that more and more distressed and disgusted my mind and heart. I had dug too deep and found too much that stank. Why rake up long-past days and long-past wrongs, then? Because they are present ones and may well grow even further into the future. The many tragedies of South Africa lie in wait, to be added to those we already know.

We must remember on what our once-high prosperity was based, and who suffered, unrecognised, to provide that prosperity. At the time of Federation, the Australia that assembled itself from those fractious colonies was one of the most prosperous countries in the world. 'Marvellous Melbourne', built on some of the wealthiest goldfields in the world (now exhausted), New South Wales with its history of sheep breeding and wool exports as well as gold, and the rest of the colonies all depended on land – land which was not ours to use. The Act of State which swept Australia into the lap of Empire could nowadays be challenged as a simple exercise of 'might over right' – and is indeed open to that accusation now that a new view is being taken by the United Nations treaties on human rights and liberties.

In 1992 I was asked by an interviewer for a literary journal in

England whether I thought Australian women were fitted for the role of 'emotional custodians' which they seemed sometimes to have taken on. It wasn't an easy question to answer, but referring to the special situation as between the indigenous peoples and their invaders, I was at least able to instance a few well-known peacemakers like Daisy Bates, the less well known Olive Pink, and a few others I knew of who had been able to act as shields, helpers and interpreters between the two antagonists – 'Western civilisation' and the 'primitive rural pests' whom they had displaced.

I still think that, in spite of many and saddening exceptions, this has been true of more women than men.

CONTRIBUTORS

Teresa Ashforth gained her PhD from Murdoch University where she teaches in human communications. Her thesis examined the way police and Aboriginal people communicate.

Kim Beazley was Minister for Education in the Whitlam Government. He retired as the Member for Fremantle in 1977. Before entering Parliament he was a teacher.

Catherine H Berndt gained her PhD at the London School of Economics. She is a foundation member of the Australian Institute of Aboriginal and Islander Studies. With her late husband Ronald she wrote about forty books on anthropology.

Geoffrey Bolton studied history at Oxford and The University of Western Australia (UWA). He has taught at UWA and Queensland University. He delivered the ABC's 1992 Boyer lectures and is now a professor at Edith Cowan University.

Veronica Brady gained her PhD from Toronto University. A Loreto nun, she is an associate professor in the Department of English at UWA.

Bill Bunbury is a social history broadcaster and author with ABC Radio National. He has taught broadcasting in remote Australia and overseas. He was previously a high school teacher.

Fred Chaney was Minister for Aboriginal Affairs in the Fraser Government. He retired in 1993 and is now at UWA. Before entering Parliament he was a lawyer.

Ted Egan is a member of the Council for Aboriginal Reconciliation. After leaving the Northern Territory Public Service where he worked as a patrol officer he became a nationally recognised singer-songwriter.

Duncan Graham is the Western Australian correspondent for the *Age* and the *Sydney Morning Herald*.

Hal Jackson was appointed President of the Western Australian Children's Court in 1989. He is also a judge of the District Court of Western Australia.

Robert Juniper is an internationally recognised artist whose arid-zone landscapes hang in many public galleries. He studied in Britain and has taught art in high schools.

Victoria Laurie is a freelance journalist and broadcaster who has worked for the ABC and SBS, and now writes for the *Bulletin*.

Bruce Petty is a cartoonist with the *Age*. He has worked in Britain and America and is widely regarded as one of Australia's most outstanding black-and-white cartoonists and innovative film-makers.

Diana Simmonds is the arts and features editor of the *Bulletin*. She came to Australia from Kenya, via Britain, in 1985.

Myrna Tonkinson gained her PhD at the University of Oregon. She has been involved in land claims in the Northern Territory and now teaches anthropology at UWA.

Judith Wright is an internationally acclaimed poet and author. Her work has been recognised with honorary degrees from several Australian universities.

FURTHER READING

This list makes no claim to being exclusive. It's little more than a small smorgasbord of recommended texts. Some have been mentioned by the contributors. Others have helped shape my philosophy. Those marked * are highly recommended.

D G

Berndt, R M and C H, *Arnhem Land: Its History and its People*, Cheshire, Melbourne, 1954.

Berndt, R M and C H, *End of an Era*, Aboriginal Studies Press, Canberra, 1989.
>   Useful background to the pastoral conditions highlighted in Chapter 14.

Berndt, R M and C H, with J E Stanton, *A World that Was*, Melbourne University Press, Melbourne, 1993.

* Berndt, R M and C H, *The World of the First Australians*, Lansdowne, Sydney, 1981.
>   This is the essential text to gain a clear and accurate understanding of traditional Aboriginal life.

* Blainey, Geoffrey, *The Triumph of the Nomads*, Macmillan, Melbourne, 1975.
>   Before he became the darling of the New Right, Professor Blainey wrote about Aboriginal history with admiration and understanding. This book is his triumph.

Bropho, Robert, *Fringedweller*, Alternative Publishing, Sydney, 1980.
   An angry and difficult book to read but worth trying because it's an authentic voice. Read in conjunction with Teresa Ashforth's essay.

Chi, Jimmy, *Bran Nue Dae*, Magabala Books, Broome, 1991.
   The book of the musical which has helped many Australians reappraise their view of Aboriginal Australia.

Davis, Jack, *The Dreamers*, Currency Press, Sydney, 1982.
   Excellent account of the anguish, oppression (and humour) of the Noongars earlier this century.

* Elkin, Adolphus, *Aboriginal Men of High Degree*, University of Queensland Press, St Lucia, 1977.
   Reveals a small part of the magic and power which existed in traditional Aboriginal culture, and still thrives in surprising places.

* Flood, Josephine, *Archaeology of the Dreamtime*, Collins, Sydney, 1983.
   A superb account of Australian pre-history written for the layperson. Essential for a clear comprehension of this country's past.

Gilbert, Kevin (ed.), *Inside Black Australia*, Penguin, Ringwood, 1988.

Gilbert, Kevin, *Because a White Man'll Never Do It*, Angus & Robertson, Sydney, 1973.
   Written with strength and feeling, these two books have done much to help non-Aboriginal readers appreciate the depth of experience and passion inside Aboriginal Australia.

Graham, Duncan, *Dying Inside*, Allen & Unwin, Sydney, 1989.
   Examines the issues which resulted in the Royal Commission into Aboriginal Deaths in Custody.

Haebich, Anna, *For Their Own Good*, University of Western Australia Press, Perth, 1988.
   A solid and dispassionate examination of the thinking and legislation of this century which inevitably led to the distress and conflict of today.

* Hardy, Frank, *The Unlucky Australians*, Nelson, Sydney, 1968.
  One of the great modern accounts of Aboriginal people shaking off oppression. A book of passion from a man who believed in an egalitarian Australia.

Harris, Stewart, *It's Coming Yet*, Aboriginal Treaty Committee, Canberra, 1979.
  In the late 1970s a small group of eminent Australians, including Judith Wright, Charles Rowley, Bill Stanner and Dr 'Nugget' Coombs, stirred the nation's conscience with a treaty proposal. The idea eventually drowned in the mire of political inaction. For more details see Judith Wright (below).

* Hawke, Steve and Gallagher, Michael, *Noonkanbah: Whose Land, Whose Law*, Fremantle Arts Centre Press, Fremantle 1989.
  A powerful contemporary account of the lengths a State Government will take to impose its will against an indigenous minority.

* Herbert, Xavier, *Capricornia*, Angus & Robertson, Sydney, 1938.
  Don't be put off by the date, this book is still in print. A fine Australian classic, written by a man tortured by the moral corruption and injustice he found in the Northern Territory.

Hutchison, D E (ed.), *Aboriginal Progress: A New Era?*, University of Western Australia Press, Perth, 1969.
  Essays which reflect the optimism generated by the 1967 Federal Referendum

Jacobs, Pat, *Mister Neville*, Fremantle Arts Centre Press, Fremantle, 1990.
  A biography of A O Neville, Chief Protector of Aboriginies in Western Australia in the 1920s and 30s. Read in association with Anna Haebich's history.

Keneally, Thomas, *The Chant of Jimmy Blacksmith*, Penguin, Ringwood, 1973
  A novel of Aboriginal revenge on white employers.

King, Michael(ed.), *Pakeha*, Penguin, Auckland, 1991.
  See the introduction to *Being Whitefella*.

Leakey, Richard, *The Making of Mankind*, Michael Joseph, London, 1981.

McLeod, Don, *How the West was Lost*, Nomads, Guildford, 1984.
Useful background to Chapters 9 and 10. Also check Donald Stuart's *Yandy*.

Morgan, Sally, *My Place*, Fremantle Arts Centre Press, Fremantle, 1987.

Reynolds, Henry, *The Other Side of the Frontier*, Penguin, Ringwood, 1982.

Reynolds, Henry, *Dispossession*, Allen & Unwin, Sydney, 1989.
Henry Reynolds' research has created a new understanding of contact history, shaking many preconceived ideas. His books are accessible and challenging.

* Rijavec, Frank, *Exile and the Kingdom*, Linfield, Film Australia, 1993.
A two-hour film which tells the story of the Roebourne people's resilience in the face of dispossession, oppression and government indifference.

Rowley, Charles, *Outcasts in White Australia*, Penguin, Ringwood, 1972.
A man ahead of his time, Professor Rowley's research and writing established a solid body of historical fact to build an understanding of black-white relations.

Spencer, Baldwin, *The Aboriginal Photographs of Baldwin Spencer*, Currey O'Neil, Melbourne, 1982
Astonishing pictures taken early this century, from central and northern Australia.

Stannage, Charles Thomas (Tom) (ed.), *A New History of Western Australia*, University of Western Australia Press, Perth, 1981.
Includes some excellent essays from writers who reject the gentrification of history.

* Stanner, William, *White Man got no Dreaming*, Australian National University Press, Canberra, 1979.
Like Charles Rowley, an author ahead of his time. Unlike so many academics, Bill Stanner can write. His essays, full of 'intellectual vitality' start in 1938. More than half a century has passed but his analyses remain relevant.

* Strehlow, Theodor, *Journey to Horseshoe Bend*, Angus & Robertson, Sydney, 1969.
   A moving account of missionary life and pastoral attitudes in the Northern Territory, and a tragic journey to seek aid for a dying man.

Strehlow, Theodor, *Songs of Central Australia*, Angus & Robertson, Sydney, 1971.
   Hard to find, but worth the effort. A brilliant and intellectual analysis of Aboriginal culture together with songs and stories equal to any from European myth.

Stuart, Donald, *Yandy*, Georgian House, Melbourne, 1959.
   A more literary account of the Aboriginal strike. See also Don McLeod's *How the West was Lost*.

Wells, Edgar, *Reward and Punishment in Arnhem Land*, Australian Institute of Aboriginal Studies, Canberra 1982.
   Useful for a detailed account of the power of mining companies. Also includes information on the Yirrkala bark painting petition. (see Chapter 9).

* Wright, Judith, *The Cry for the Dead*, Oxford University Press, Melbourne, 1981.
   One of Australia's most outstanding poets, Judith Wright wrote powerfully of the despoilation of her country and the maltreatment of the First Australians. Her voice has been respected by those who would otherwise remain indifferent because her credentials are establishment and pastoral.

Wright, Judith, *We Call for a Treaty*, Fontana, Sydney, 1985.
   Vital for an understanding of the thinking and response to the treaty proposals.